REAL SHORT STORIES

RICHARD STOEBEL

Published by Hallard Press LLC. www.HallardPress.com

Publisher's Cataloging-in-Publication Data

Names: Stoebel, Richard, author.
Title: Real short stories / Richard Stoebel.
Description: The Villages, FL: Hallard Press, 2024.
Identifiers: LCCN: 2024915021 | ISBN: 978-1-962326-39-1 (paperback) | 978-1-962326-40-7 (ebook)
Subjects: LCSH Stoebel, Richard. | United States--Social life and customs--20th century--Anecdotes. | BISAC BIOGRAPHY & AUTOBIOGRAPHY / Memoirs
Classification: LCC E169.Z83 .S86 2024 | DDC 814.6--dc23

978-1-962326-39-1 (paperback)
978-1-962326-40-7 (ebook)

CONTENTS

In Memoriam

John W. Prince
1942 – 2023

John was a founder and partner of Hallard Press LLC. He passed away after a year of treatment for terminal brain cancer.

John was a guiding factor in the publishing of my first two books. I considered him a good friend. He will be sorely missed as I have my third book published using "lessons learned" from my association with him.

May he rest in peace.

Richard Stoebel

Acknowledgments

Thanks to my wife, Brenda, for love and encouragement in allowing me to express myself in books and in every day life. She is my wife of 55 years and best friend.

Thanks to God for giving me good health and the memory to recall both good and bad events from the past. Hopefully, we learn from these experiences so that we don't repeat the bad ones.

Thanks to Chris and Pat Beltrami for their guidance and expertise with the photo images on the covers and in the body of this book. We consider them as "best friends."

Thanks to Victoria Harding-Wakeen for editing all of my grammatical errors and to Nancy Hellekson of Hallard Press for guidance in publishing this book.

An Introduction

In my lifetime I have been witness to a plethora of extreme happiness, frightening tragedies, and pretty much everything in between. I have lived what I consider a normal life, given all the paths I could have chosen. In spite of my shortcomings, which we all have but many will not admit to, I have seen and done some interesting things. All without having killed myself, I might add. Some luck along the way might have been a factor and some calculated risks might have also been a factor. I'm quite sure of that.

It all started quite literally with my parents, who were hardworking people of German heritage. That makes me and my sister, Beverly, full-blooded German if there actually is such a thing as "full-blooded." Ancestry and 123 & Me searches confirm a European background with even a titch of Neanderthal somewhere in the past! That might account for some of the unexplained and brute decisions I have occasionally made during my lifetime.

My parents were factory workers. Henry, my dad, worked in the textile industry. His parents, when they immigrated from Germany to the United States in the late 1800s, came from a textile trade background, so this may have influenced why my dad gravitated to that type of work. Having to quit school at the age of thirteen after the loss of his father in an accident, he went to work doing various jobs to help support his mother and the family. Although he didn't have a formal higher education, he learned his skills from the school of hard knocks and good old common sense. He and my mother, Flora, went on to make a good life working together and having a family. They even built their own house. We always had clean clothes to wear, and we never went hungry. Welfare was a dirty word back in those days, so hard work and persistence paid the bills.

My mother was dedicated to raising a family and providing a steady environment for us to be brought up in. She and my dad were a good team, always pulling in the same direction. They were not always in harmony with each other and disagreed on a variety of issues. But, in the end, they would find common ground and move on with the task at hand... making the best living that they could and raising a family. While we were young, Mother picked up odd jobs to bring in a little extra money. I remember her cleaning neighborhood houses while we youngsters occupied ourselves with games or toys. Later, when we were teenagers in school, she gained employment at a pocketbook factory in town. That's when most things were still made here in the United States and not overseas. She ended her working career doing piece work at the RAYOVAC battery and flashlight factory in our town of Clinton, Massachusetts. That money was used to help pay for my formal college education. I will be eternally grateful for the exceptional support of my mother and father, without which I could not have accomplished all the things I have in life.

This book is a compilation of short vignettes about various events and happenings during my lifetime. All the stories are real, not fiction. Hence, the name of the book 'Real Short Stories.' I present them in no particular order, but they might rather be classified as the good old days, the mid-life days, and recent events. I think it's kinda funny how the mind works. I can remember so many vivid details from the 'old days' but can't remember what happened just yesterday. Old memories keep flooding back, so they must have left a good, or really bad, impression on me to remember all of the dirty details. Some of these stories might be found interesting to readers. They also might be found funny, scary, informative, unbelievable, or even tragic. In any event, read on to see some of the things I had to deal with in my life. I believe that everyone has a story to tell. This is mine and I am sharing some, but not all, of the gory details!

Scouts' Honor

As a young boy, I was always drawn to the outdoors, probably because of my dad. I loved fishing and hunting. That is probably why I got into scouting. It started with Cub Scouts. My mother got involved and headed up a den which is usually comprised of a small group of kids from the neighborhood. There was a handbook with guidelines on what it takes to become a scout. Of course, there was the obligatory uniform, levels of advancement and the earning of merit badges along the way. The badges could have something to do with outdoor activities like camping and fishing. Shooting at such an early age was probably not one of the options. That would come later when you were old enough to join the Boy Scouts. Other badges might include civic duties, school, church, hiking, nature, sciences, first aid, sports, and more.

Around the age of eleven, I advanced to Boy Scouts. I was quite active in the monthly meetings and camping at various places both in the summer and winter. One winter, I participated in a 'freezeout' adventure. I think it was held in January or February. We were taught some of the techniques to stay warm during the night, but I must have missed that presentation because I could not sleep and ended up sitting in front of the campfire all night! It was freaking cold, and I never did get a wink of sleep. I think that is why, in later years, I never really embraced camping. The memory of that experience left an indelible mark on me that never went away. Give me a nice, warm hotel room any day!!

One of the experiences I had the next summer was a one-day hiking trip with another new Boy Scout who also happened to be a distant cousin of mine. We were led by an older teenage scout. It was just the three of us on this fishing adventure. We hiked to a small stream which was probably a mile or two from our house. We did some fishing but never caught anything and that was okay because we were just out to have a nice day. Those sandwiches that my mom prepared for us sure came in handy. As the day progressed into early afternoon, our lead scout said, "I've got a surprise for you. Kneel down over here." Being gullible kids, we did as we were told. "Close your eyes," which we did, never suspecting anything wrong. When we were told to open our eyes, our scout leader was standing in front of us exposing himself. I froze. I knew instinctively that this was wrong in so many ways. After a few minutes, which felt like a lifetime, he said, "If you're not going to do anything, I'll just put this bad boy away." I was numb as we packed up our things and headed home.

I'm not sure if this incident bothered my cousin as much as it bothered me. After all, he was the kid who stole candy bars from a local mom-and-pop grocery store while I was with him.

My conscience kicked in and I told my parents. They took me back to the grocery store to confess what had happened. The owner was so impressed with my honesty that he grabbed a candy bar and gave it to me for free because I told the truth. One of life's lessons that I will always remember.

It wasn't a day or two later that my conscience kicked in again and I told my parents what had happened during the Boy Scout day hike. That was all my parents had to hear because my dad accompanied me to the next scout meeting. The head scout leader, an adult, listened to my story in private and instantly reacted by questioning the senior scout whom I had accused of doing this lewd act. Without hesitation, the senior scout was told to pack up his things and leave, never to return. I'm not sure if his parents were ever informed of this incident, but this guy was definitely a pedophile in the making. I remember his name to this day, but I've decided to spare his family any embarrassment. I often wondered how many other victims this guy affected during his lifetime and how he and/or his family might have come to grips with it. I'll never know and it's probably best that way. I urge you to protect your children and grandchildren from these kinds of things. There's probably more of this going on than we can possibly imagine.

I advanced to the rank of Life Scout but never continued to the highest rank of Eagle Scout. As a young teenager, school, cars, girls and work (not necessarily in that order) got in the way. I lost interest in scouting by this point in life. It was time to move on.

As of this writing, Boy Scouts of America has been renamed. After 115 years, it will now be known as Scouting

America. The change was the result of a $2 billion dollar settlement to former scouts who were sexually abused. I was not part of that lawsuit but I can certainly identify with the problem. The changes were also meant to modernize the organization to be more inclusive. Girls were allowed to join the Boy Scouts (Scouts USA) in 2019. The first female Eagle Scout was ordained in 2020. I don't think I'm the first to be disappointed in these changes because I still believe that there are two distinct genders, boys and girls. I don't go along with the inclusion and transgender crap that is being taught to our children in schools these days. Look at sports where men transition to women and then compete against them. It's tragic and never should have been allowed to happen in the first place. Give me the good old days, thank you very much. God bless us in this time of turmoil. I predict that the misguided woke community is due for a "correction."

Farms

I was fortunate as a young lad to get my first real job at a farm. It was an apple orchard in Bolton, Massachusetts, owned by a retired Dr. Clemens. My first job at the orchard was picking up apples from the ground to be brought to the cider mill. I graduated the next year to picking from the trees. I wasn't as fast as the Nova Scotia migrant workers who were hired, but I still did pretty well. "Handle them like eggs, only faster," as the foreman would say. The next year, when I was about 15 years old, I was allowed to start driving some of the farm machinery, including an old International W4 tractor, a bulldozer, and a couple of flatbed trucks. This is where I learned to drive. There were a couple of times that I could have, and probably should have, been killed, but I was lucky. Somebody upstairs was looking after me. I've learned that many farmers have missing fingers from the errant handling of sickle bars, farm machinery, and the like. My injuries, thankfully, were less severe.

One of my favorite activities at the orchard was when a Piper Pawnee agricultural airplane flew in to spray the young crop of apples in the late summer, probably with the now-banned DDT! I and another kid held the long flag poles to mark the rows to be sprayed. That pilot flew so low that his landing gear hit the top branches of the trees. Some of the spray mist rained down on us. We didn't know or worry about toxins back in those days. We were oblivious to the harm it could cause. We also handled other poisons like zinc phosphate, which was used to kill mice. We never paid too much attention to long-term health effects back then, so I marvel at the fact that I am still alive today. Go figure. The neighboring farm was a peach orchard. When crops were ripe, we would sneak over to grab a peach at lunchtime. The peach orchard workers sneaked over to grab an apple. This was a normal daily occurrence.

Another farm just up the road from the orchard was a Morgan/Holstein ranch owned by a Boston lawyer and his wife. I hung out there quite a bit. What was the attraction? Pretty young twin girls by the name of Betty and Bonnie! Betty was my first real heartthrob. Let's just say that there's a lot to love about farm girls. The owner of the ranch trained Morgan horses to pull carriages and had won a whole office full of trophies and blue ribbons. I accompanied the ranch team to a couple of shows as an extra hand. One day back at the farm, as a storm approached, I was drafted to help get the horses into the barn. As I held two of them by their halters, we headed to the barn. The horses were spooked when lightning struck nearby with the resultant thunder, and they started to run. I couldn't hold them back, so I just went into a tuck, held on for dear life, and hoped for the best. They turned the corner together at the rear of the stables and stopped when they got inside. I was just glad they didn't go in two different directions. Man, I didn't know two horsepower could be that powerful.

Because Holsteins are milk cows, they have to be artificially inseminated to produce a heifer. This process keeps the milk flowing. One cold day, I witnessed a veterinarian sticking his gloved hand up the back end of one of the cows. When he pulled his hand out, the steam vapors evaporated off his arm. It took me a while to figure out this was the insemination method. I can unequivocally say that I have never personally stuck my arm up a cow's ass, and I'm proud of it.

Of course, there can't be calves without a bull. This ranch had one. He was big, and he was mean. I was sitting on the bull fence with Betty's older brother one day when the bull approached us. With a quick motion, the brother grabbed the nose ring, jumped into the corral, and started to twist. The bull's head kept contorting until the body followed the motion, and before I knew it, the big boy was on the ground. As soon as the bull was down, the brother jumped up and quickly climbed over the fence. That big bull was mad and looking for revenge. I had never seen anything quite like that in my young life and never desired to try a stunt like that myself.

I helped, from time to time, to load bales of hay onto a truck and a conveyor belt. That is hard, dirty work, but the girls worked right along with us. Farm girls are tough. I was hanging out with Betty one day near an electrified fence. She said, "Go ahead and touch it. It won't hurt you." Hell, I'd do anything if she dared me to, so I grabbed the wire. I learned the shocking truth in a heartbeat! She said, "Watch this," and proceeded to grab and hold onto the wire. Guess I'm not so tough after all.

Another memory of my time at the ranch was when Betty and I were sitting on the stone wall surrounding one of the Morgan pastures. A couple of horses were grazing behind us while we talked. Without warning, one of the horses came up behind me and bit me on the shoulder. Holy shit, let me tell you… that hurt! The horse must have been in a bad mood and took it out on me. Note to self: Be more careful in the future around horses while being distracted by a pretty farm girl.

Schools

I was born and raised in the small industrial town of Clinton, Massachusetts. Actually, our house was in Clinton but the garage, merely 20 feet away, was in the town of Bolton. My parents paid taxes in both towns. If I had lived in Bolton, I could have gone to the smaller schools in that town and, eventually, the Nashoba Regional High School. But it was ordained that I would go to the Clinton school system because it was more local.

The first public school I attended for grades 1 through 5 was Bowers Elementary on Water Street. We walked to school from our house each day. The school was probably about a mile away and, of course, it was uphill in both directions! There were no school buses in those days so you either walked or got a ride from somebody. Since we had only one car at the time and my dad commuted to Worcester for his job, my sister and I walked daily. We were kinda like a mailman. In the wind, rain, sleet, or snow... the mail must go through! We didn't mind it, though, because we didn't know any other way. The first and second-grade rooms were on the first floor, and the third, fourth, and fifth on the second floor. Fourth and fifth grades were combined under Miss Flaherty. I must have been a teacher's pet because I was asked on a couple of occasions to go down to the first-grade room and help out that teacher when she wasn't feeling good. One of my favorite remembrances in the fifth grade was fire drills. The boys clamored down the fire escape at the back of the building first. If we got a head start, we'd watch the girls come down the open staircase next. We had a nice view looking up their skirts. Boys will be boys!

From the neighborhood schools, we moved on to the 6th, 7[th,] and 8th grades in various buildings near the center of town. One kid who was a little on the wild side pestered me at recess from time to time. He'd put me into a headlock or just push me around for his amusement. He was bigger and older than me and I suspect he was held back a grade or two. He had cigarette breath which was disgusting. One day I had had enough of this guy. I was a lover, not a fighter, and didn't go looking for fights. But this time, I just felt compelled to haul off and punch him in the face. Down he went. I never had a problem with him again. He probably went looking for someone else to bully and gave up on me.

Our high school was located nearby and right across from the town park. When I was 16, I had my driver's license and a $50 car. I used to park it near the stone pillar fence around the park's perimeter. I lent my car to a classmate once (dumb move), and he crashed into one of those pillars, damaging the right front fender. So, it was off to the junkyard to get a used fender. I replaced the fender myself and learned a lesson from this experience. Note to self: Never lend your car to a so-called friend.

The main part of the high school burned down just before I was to attend as a freshman. We went to classes in the remaining part of the school as well as the armory and grade schools nearby until a new school could be built at another location in town. High school students started early in the morning and were done each day by noon. Grammar school kids then attended classes in some of the same buildings from noon to five PM. I liked this arrangement because I could work a job in the afternoon and earn some money.

Eventually, the new high school was completed, and we were the first seniors to graduate from it — the Class of 1962. I was one of eight students in the technical program, which included higher levels of physics, chemistry, and calculus. I never liked calculus and always thought "What the hell am I going to use this for?" And, true to form, my prophecy was right. I never used it again in my lifetime!

My early education in the public school system must have been adequate enough because eventually, I graduated from a two-year technical school, Wentworth Institute, in Boston and an engineering school in California, Northrop Institute. Both great schools. I do have some stories to share about those schools, but I will save that for another chapter.

NITWIT

In 1962, I attended Wentworth Institute of Technology (WIT) in Boston at the urging of my high school guidance counselor. At the time, it was a two-year technical school concentrating in electrical, mechanical, civil, and aeronautical certificated and associate degree programs. Years later, it offered Bachelor of Science degrees in these same fields. I paid for my first semester out of savings that I had accumulated, thanks to my mother who saw the wisdom of putting money aside for a rainy day.

During my two years in the big city of Boston, I had some interesting experiences. Besides studying, we ventured beyond the campus to meet girls from Boston, Simmons, and Northeastern Universities. Of course, there were the occasional panty raids and parties which were all part of college life. You did have to be careful where and when you went out because there were some dangerous places to avoid. You never went to the Roxbury area of the city because it was filled with gangs that, for some reason, didn't like college kids. Out alone at night was also something to be avoided. A fellow student who played a mean guitar was coming home through Fenway Park one evening after a gig. He was jumped by a gang of hoodlums, beat up, and had his prized guitar stolen. He was hurt so bad, having been hit or kicked in the head, that he had to leave school. I'm not sure if he was ever able to return. Being vigilant, I survived the big city and went on to graduate from WIT.

After working at Pratt & Whitney Aircraft Engines in East Hartford, Connecticut for a couple of years, I decided to go back to school. My reasoning was that I could double my salary by earning a Bachelor of Science degree. I applied to Embry Riddle in Florida, Parks Institute, which at the time was located in St. Louis, and Northrop Institute of Technology in California (NIT). NIT responded to my inquiry the quickest and offered me the most credits from my previous studies, so it was off to California for me. I enrolled in the Aircraft Maintenance Engineering program. The college ran on a quarterly semester schedule, so I would be able to graduate with my BS degree in less than two years. I loved living in California. The warm, dry weather agreed with me, and I was able to get around using a motorcycle that I picked up for a few bucks and rebuilt. The lady who owned the apartment complex I was living in befriended me and made me the building manager for a reduction in rent. I collected rent payments from my roommates and all the other people living there. At the front of the complex was a larger two-bedroom unit that was rented to a couple and their kids. I wouldn't see them very often and after a couple of rent collections, they stopped paying. They were eventually evicted and when the landlady and I entered the unit, it was quite literally trashed. The place was filthy with trash everywhere, grease in and on the stove and holes in the walls. One of the kids must have had a mental problem because one of the bedrooms had ripped-up papers and magazines all over the place. I helped restore the apartment for future rental. After experiencing this, I think it is the reason that I never wanted to be a rental property owner in my lifetime. There are some nasty people out there.

There are lots of stories to be told about my time in California. One of my Hawaiian roommates got the hots to buy a handgun for some reason. When he got it back to the apartment, he was afraid to shoot it, so I volunteered to help. We set up a phone book in the bathroom, loaded a 9mm cartridge into the chamber, and fired one shot down the hallway into the target. Fortunately, I hit the target, and the bullet did not penetrate the thick book. The noise was deafening. We were crazy kids for doing this inside an apartment, but hey, we were young, dumb, and full of c__, as the saying goes. I had another roommate who was a daredevil. He once jumped off the 2nd story roof into the pool. He survived. On another occasion, we were having a big party at the apartment complex. A student who was drunk and didn't like me for some reason took a swing at me at the urging of some other guys. I ducked and he punched the wall behind me, breaking his hand. Geez, what was that all about? I'm a lover, not a fighter, and I usually try to avoid these situations.

Eventually, I graduated from NIT and got a job in the experimental engineering department back at Pratt. This is where I would meet my future wife, Brenda, and enjoy a 43-year career with the company. Life is good. Because I graduated from both NIT and WIT, I could identify as a NITWIT. I'm okay with that. I've been called worse!

TIJUANA

While going to college in southern California, it was inevitable that I would go across the border to Tijuana, Mexico. It was almost a right of passage for college guys to make the trip for, let's say, the cultural experience. One of my roommates, Bob, volunteered to drive us down there in his black 57 Chevy convertible. Another roommate, myself, and a classmate from Alaska jumped in the car for the day trip and headed south. Tijuana was about 140 miles and just over two hours away along Interstate 5. We could make it even faster if we put the pedal to the metal. We drove through San Juan Capistrano which is famous for swallows migrating and returning there each spring. In fact, the birds return with such regularity that a festival is held in March to celebrate the occasion. In our haste to get to Mexico, we must have been going a little bit over the speed limit because a state trooper put his lights on and pulled us over. We were issued a speeding ticket, which we would either have to come back to pay on a specific court date or we could go directly to the courthouse and pay it right then. We opted to pay then and headed into town. We didn't have a lot of money with us, being college students, but we all dug deep into our pockets and paid the fine. There were no credit cards back then (1966) and none of us had a checkbook, so the fine had to be paid in cash.

After this delay, we resumed our trip south, trying to stay within the speed limit. We couldn't afford another ticket. Once across the border and into Tijuana, we started to explore the town. We were warned by other students who had been here not to jaywalk because, if caught, there would be a fine for that. If you couldn't pay, you would be put in jail. Our first stop was to the Jai Alai Fronton Palacio to watch a game. It was the first time I had ever witnessed the game of Jai Alai. I remember that the restrooms were manned by attendants who gave us dirty looks when we didn't tip them. We just didn't have the money for that. We had lunch at a small sidewalk taco bar. It was the first time I ever ate a taco and I really took a liking to them. Rumor had it that they used meat from feral cats for the tacos. I'm not sure if that was true but I gotta admit that, after eating a few, I had this strange feeling come over me to lift my leg and lick myself. Just saying.

We went to a bar, which turned out to be a stripper joint. We were seated at a table next to the stage, where we ordered drinks. It didn't matter that we were still teenagers. We got served anyway. It wasn't long before the music started and the stage lights came on. A pretty young Mexican girl strutted her stuff and started to remove the few articles of clothing she had on. For some reason, she made her way over to me. I was seated right next to the stage. She must have thought I was cute or, more likely, gullible. I had never seen anything like this before, so I nervously lit up a cigarette and tried not to look. The lit cigarette was removed from my lips and, after a moment, was returned to my mouth. I quickly figured out that the cigarette more than likely had gone to "East Jabrew," but I couldn't be certain. We watched the rest of the show and left. I secretly hoped that I wouldn't contract a disease from this encounter or that my lips wouldn't fall off sometime in the future.

In the evening, we got something to eat. Hopefully, it wasn't cat food this time. We had a few beers in another bar and when nature called, we looked for a bathroom. As it turns out, the bathroom was a trough in the middle of the bar room. And there were women bar-tenders and waitresses. Oh well, when in Rome, do as the Romans do. When you gotta go, you gotta go. This was definitely a learning experience for me. We headed back to the car for the drive home to Inglewood, California. We passed another bar that was down a side street. There were a bunch of drunk Mexicans hanging around outside. For some reason, the Alaskan kid we had with us felt the urge to yell out to them, "REMEMBER THE ALAMO!" You stupid fool, you're gonna get us killed! The drunks started chasing us and we ran for it. It was probably the fastest I had ever run in my life. If it had been a 5K, I would have won the gold medal. Somehow, we made it back to the car and got the hell out of there without getting shot, knifed, beat up, or all of the above. I was happy to escape with my life. Looking back at this adventure, I realize how foolish we all were and I'm still really glad that my lips never fell off.

DRONES

When I was a kid, I fell in love with airplanes. A neighborhood young man down the street from us learned to fly at a local airport nearby. He buzzed his parents at low altitude and always flew over our house at chimney-top altitude. I thought this was pretty cool, so I started to build model airplanes at a little work area in the basement of my parents' house. When I was a little older, I started flying gas-powered models in our field behind the house. These small planes were controlled by a pair of lines, connected at one end by a U-shaped handle and at the other by a bellcrank working the elevator. We flew them in circles and performed maneuvers like loops, wingovers, and inverted flight. This is where I developed my rudimentary understanding of how an airplane works. As a reminder, I have a poster displayed in my man-cave garage that pretty much describes how I felt all those years ago. The poster shows a young boy working on a model and reads, "ONCE UPON A TIME THERE WAS A BOY WHO REALLY LOVED AIRPLANES. IT WAS ME. THE END."

As time went on, I witnessed an agricultural Piper Pawnee airplane that sprayed the apple orchard trees where I was working part-time. It was cool to watch the low-level antics of this pilot at work. Even the spray that misted down on us didn't matter. We were not worried about toxic poisoning back in those days. I went on to get my early aviation training as a mechanic and worked for Pratt & Whitney Aircraft Engines in East Hartford, Connecticut. After a short stint there, I went back to school to get my Bachelor of Science degree in the aeronautical field, and then it was back to Pratt where I worked in the Experimental Test Engineering department. This is where I met my wife, Brenda. We got married, bought our first house together, and started a family. I had obtained my private pilot's license by this time and owned a 1946 Piper J3C65 Cub. I rebuilt and modified the plane by clipping seven feet off the wingspan. This made it more aerobatic. Working on the Cub was just like playing with models, only bigger.

Over the years, I continued to play with model airplanes. I have progressed from control line models to radio-controlled types flown with a transmitter and a receiver. You'd think that learning to fly a radio-controlled airplane would be easy, having flown full-size aircraft, but the technique takes a while to learn because you are not actually in the pilot's seat. The electronics are actually telemetry systems that precisely control the aircraft. Earlier attempts at this hobby used frequencies that could be interfered with by truckers' CB radios or other aircraft. With the latest technology, narrow-band frequencies bind the radio to the airplane reducing interference from other sources. Along with this advanced technology came the proliferation of drones.

I had a small one that I flew inside the house and trained our grandkids to fly when they visited. These drones have now become so advanced that they are used by police departments, professional photographers, and the military. They can be flown as an FPV (first-person view) where you control flight from an onboard camera, just as if you were actually seated in the drone. They can be programmed to automatically land on the same spot they took off from when batteries get low. They occasionally fly into restricted airspace, interfering with operational aircraft. Therein lies the problem. Because of this, the FAA got involved and rules regulating these aircraft started to become more complex.

What started out as an innocent backyard hobby has now turned into a highly regulated sport. Radio control airplanes and drones of a half-pound or more in weight are now required to be registered with the FAA and have a transponder on board just like a full-size aircraft. The transponder transmits signals to ATC (air traffic control) at nearby airports so that airplane traffic can be safely identified and controlled. Flying model airplanes is still fun, but some of the fun has been reduced because of regulations being levied on the sport. I suppose it's a necessary evil in today's society. I, personally, liked "the good old days."

A poster in my garage pretty much describes how I felt about airplanes from an early age. I've been told that the boy looks exactly like I did when I was young. Just saying.

FLYING

There is something about airplanes that has intrigued me from a young age. My earliest recollection was when I was about ten or twelve years old. On my bicycle, riding along a country road in central Massachusetts, I heard an airplane. I looked up to watch this beautiful machine flying overhead and could not take my eyes off it. The next thing I knew, I had driven off the pavement and into the bushes at the side of the road! I guess I was intrigued with airplanes right from the beginning. As it turns out, this was the beginning of a lifelong passion. In my old age, I still look up to watch everything flying overhead, whether it is an airplane, helicopter, or hot air balloon. If it's flying, it's got my attention.

At an early age, I built and flew control line airplanes with small gas engines. Then, at my high school guidance counselor's suggestion, I went to Wentworth Institute in Boston for the Aircraft Maintenance program. Upon graduation with my airframe and powerplant training, I got a job at Pratt &

Whitney Aircraft in East Hartford, Connecticut, as a mechanic in the experimental assembly and test department. It was a great job but it was also the first time I ever had to punch a time clock, which I hated. This led to a salary job as an engineering aide, which was more favorable to me.

After a couple of years at Pratt, I realized if I got my bachelor's degree, I could double my salary. After applying to several schools around the country, I finally decided on Northrop Institute in Inglewood, California. The school was located on the final approach to a Los Angeles airport runway and the noise was deafening when an airplane was landing. If a professor were in the middle of a lecture, he would just stop, wait for the noise to subside, and then continue from where he left off. This was normal operating procedure for the two years I was there.

While I was going to school in California, I used extra money from side jobs to start taking flying lessons at the local Hawthorne Airport. Back then, flying was fairly cheap. You could rent a plane for $10 and an instructor for a little bit more. During my first solo after takeoff, I was diverted to a holding area because of an emergency in the pattern. I could see my flight instructor down below, wondering what the hell was going on as I flew away from the airport traffic pattern. After the emergency was over, I was directed back to the airport and landed safely. And I lived to tell you about it! Let me just say that if you ever have the chance to solo an airplane, it is an experience you will never forget. You, quite literally, have your life in your own hands. Trust me, it is much more exhilarating than driving a car, or motorcycle, or boat by yourself for the first time.

After graduation from Northrop, I got a job in Pratt's experimental engineering department. I didn't know it then, but I would have a long and exciting 43-year career with this company. I would also meet my beautiful wife there, but that is a story for another chapter. Before starting my new career, though, I took a couple of months off to work at Sterling Airport in Massachusetts and continue with my flying lessons. While there, I spotted a 1946 Piper J3C65 Cub being sold by the fixed base operator. Long story short, I bought the Cub for $1,200, worked off a portion of the cost, and paid $950 out of pocket for this old airplane. I knew it was old and needed to be recovered because I was washing it one day, and the fabric on the wings ripped. No problem. That's what duct tape is for! I flew the airplane for a time with multiple rips taped up until I had to take the airplane apart to refurbish it. There are lots of stories to tell about this chapter in my life, but I will save that for later.

I went on to obtain my private pilot's license out of Hartford Brainard Airport and continue to love flying to this day. Again, airplanes have become a lifelong passion, and I am forever grateful for all the memories associated with this field of work and recreation.

STALL

During the time that I was rebuilding my Piper Cub airplane, I had acquired my private pilot's license and was actively flying rental aircraft. I met a friend of a friend who had a farm in Coventry, Connecticut. Mike Metnoski owned a J3 Cub like mine that was currently airworthy, and he had another one that was disassembled in the barn. Mike worked in the machine shop at Pratt & Whitney but was also the quintessential gentleman farmer with cows, chickens... and a field big enough to fly out of. I flew with him from his field many times but since he was still a "student" pilot, I was always the pilot in command. At one end of his field on the north side, there was a drainage ditch. If you were taking off in that direction, you had to be airborne before the ditch which was really not a problem. When taking off to the south, there were trees. Tall trees that you had to clear. The ditch shortened the runway length in that direction. On cold days, the trees were not a problem. You could clear them by a hundred feet or more. On hot days with high humidity, it was a struggle to get over those big maple and oak trees. The flight plan was always to get the wheels off the ground, hold the airplane down with wings level to build up speed, and then pull up steeply at the last moment to clear the obstacle. We barely made it a couple of times, clearing the tops of the trees by just a few feet! I guess that's what makes flying so much fun! The thrill of victory or the agony of defeat.

My father-in-law, Joe, was a daredevil. He went flying with me on a few occasions. He would never refuse to fly. Mike let us use his airplane one beautiful summer day, so Joe and I took off for a little adventure over the central Connecticut farmlands and lakes. Joe had no formal training as a pilot but, as I mentioned, he was a daredevil and had no fear. When I handed the controls over to him he handled the Cub like a pro. With minimal instruction, he flew for over a half hour. He was in seventh heaven. Had he been given the opportunity, he would have been a great pilot. I could picture him as a WWII fighter pilot. No fear.

My wife, Brenda, flew with me from time to time. I'm not so sure she totally bought into the flying sport, but she did it to please me because she knew of my love of things with wings. We rented a Cessna 152 from the flying school at Brainard Field in Hartford. We took off and headed south toward Long Island Sound. One of our favorite areas along the shoreline was in Rhode Island. Misquamicut State Beach, Blue Shutters, Green Hill. All were beautiful and fairly deserted on this early spring day. To get a closer look and provide a thrill for Brenda, I decided to buzz the beach just offshore. As I descended, we were clipping along about a hundred feet off the beach. Brenda must have been excited because she turned to me and gave me a big hug! I said, "No, no, no. Not right now. I've got my hands full flying this close to the ground!" She didn't realize the importance of controlling the airplane at this crucial moment. When we finally gained some altitude, I accepted the hug.

On our way back to Hartford, we were cruising along at a couple thousand feet. For some reason, I got the crazy idea of demonstrating a flight maneuver that we were taught during primary training. A stall. Without communicating what we were going to do and what to expect, I reduced the throttle, carburetor heat on, pulled the nose of the airplane up, and held that attitude until the stall. Just before a full stall, the airplane gives you a little advance notice, with the wings shaking as they lose lift. Once fully stalled, the nose suddenly drops, and you look straight down. Recovery is easy. A little down elevator and some power and you are flying again. Easy peasy, except Brenda's stomach was still at the top of the stall. To say she didn't like or appreciate the beauty of this maneuver is an understatement. I'm not sure, but I think this was the last time Brenda ever flew with me. Gotta find another way to impress this girl.

JOE

My father-in-law, Alphie Adelard Gosselin, was an interesting person. He was born in 1918 and brought up in Manchester, New Hampshire. He was the second youngest of ten children. His father traveled away from home for his job and only earned a meager wage. Alphie was eleven years old when the great depression of 1929 set in and times were tough. Stealing food was sometimes the only way to sustain life and avoid going hungry. Times were so tough that he and another sibling lived for a time with Jesuit priests in an orphanage. During the 1930s, Alphie had had enough of priests and school. He lied about his age, changed his name to Joe Gosselin, and joined the Army. At the time, the minimum age to join was 21, and I'm guessing he was still a teenager when he signed up. After basic training, he was stationed in Panama. The Panama Canal was built by the United States and completed in 1914. It was a strategic location connecting the Pacific and Atlantic oceans and could be used for both military and commercial passage. At the time, the Panama Canal was considered one of the seven wonders of the world. Because of military ships passing through the canal, an army presence was required there for security purposes.

From my son-in-law perspective, Joe was easy to talk to, and I liked listening to his real-life stories. While in Panama, he was on a 20-mile hike when he contracted malaria. One of the officers was assigned to escort Joe back to the base camp. The officer was astride his horse while Joe, in delirium, was ordered to make his way back on foot. The officer never offered to give Joe a ride. Pitiful. After spending time in the camp hospital, Joe eventually recovered from his bout with malaria. As time went on during his service in Panama, Joe trained to be a golden glove boxer. He was a small man and fought in either the flyweight or lightweight class. Because of his upbringing, Joe basically had no fear of getting hurt. He did quite well in the boxing ring, winning many bouts. He was small, but fast. I know this from fooling around with him after I married his daughter. Because I had no official training as a boxer, Joe could punch my lights out and have me on the ground in no time flat. I respected him for this.

After getting married and starting a family, the USA got involved in WWII after the bombing of Pearl Harbor by the Japanese in December 1941. Joe was drafted as a 23-year-old and definitely did not want to return to the Army, so he joined the Navy. He said his goodbyes to his new wife, Bridget, and young son and went off to war. Joe was assigned to an LST (tank landing ship) carrying tanks, equipment, and troops. Joe talked about making a stop on the Hawaiian island of Oahu at Pearl Harbor. He always wanted to go back to visit or retire there but never did. The Hawaiian Islands must have left a favorable, lasting impression on him. The captain of his ship was not well-liked. Because of this, he had stops mounted on the seven 40mm and twelve 20mm anti-aircraft guns so they could not be swiveled at the ship's bridge. The captain also had a pet monkey on board by the name of Bonzo. Bonzo shit everywhere on the ship, including Joe's bunk. The men were always cleaning up after the primate. During guard duty one night while at sea, Bonzo approached Joe. Joe might have even enticed him to come closer with a treat. At the right moment, Joe grabbed the monkey by the neck... and gave him a mighty heave overboard! Bonzo might have tread water for a little while but was never seen again. Everyone wondered where the pet monkey had gone, but Joe never uttered a word for fear of reprisal. His bunk was shit-free for the rest of his tour of duty.

Navy pay was a meager $50 per month. Not a lot of money for risking one's life. His pay was sent home to his new wife and son. Joe sold most of his beer rations on board the ship to his fellow shipmates and sent that money home as well. He was a good father. At some point, his convoy was attacked by Japanese bombers and fighter aircraft. All hands on deck! Joe was assigned to one of the anti-aircraft guns and described to me his role in shooting down one of the enemy aircraft. The Japanese Zero was trying to hit his ship, kamikaze style. All guns were pointed at this one particular airplane. His gun found its mark, but Joe could not release his finger from the trigger even after the airplane crashed into the sea near his ship. The man who had no fear finally felt fear. I can only imagine what he felt at the moment. These are the real heroes in life, not the football players or actors that many people adore. During this combat, a nearby ammunition ship was hit and destroyed. The explosion was so loud that it did damage to Joe's ears, which he lived with for the rest of his life. As their LST passed by what was left of the ammunition ship, there was nothing but debris floating in the water where a big ship had just been. All men on board were lost at sea. Sad.

When Joe went away to war, his wife Bridget warned him not to get any tattoos, but that warning was ignored, and he came home sporting an eagle and Navy image on his left arm. After all he had been through, he earned the right to remember his sacrifice with a badge of honor permanently displayed on his body. Upon Joe's passing, we were able to save his honorable discharge paperwork and a picture of him in his uniform. On his right sleeve is an eagle with three stripes, indicating that he had obtained the rank of petty officer first class. We have the discharge paperwork and picture prominently displayed on the wall of our home office. It is a fitting tribute for a man who was not only in the Army, but also saw combat action in the Navy. Freedom is not free. Men like Joe are the real heroes in life.

CUB

Having my own airplane at the young age of 21 was a dream come true. Everything I had done in my early years revolved around airplanes. It all started with model making. Then I graduated to flying engine-powered control line airplanes in our backyard. I even won a July 4th flying contest at the local football/baseball field in Clinton, Massachusetts. I was getting pretty good at flying wingovers, loops, and inverted flight. Fuller Field, I just learned, is the oldest continuously operating baseball field in the United States. Go figure. Never too old to learn.

After high school, I graduated from Wentworth Institute in Boston with a two-year certificate in the aircraft maintenance program. My next two years were spent working at Pratt & Whitney Aircraft in East Hartford, Connecticut. I started as a mechanic in Experimental Assembly and Test, but I did not like punching a clock, so I transferred to a salary job as an Engineering Aide.

It didn't take me long to figure out that I could double my income by going back to school and obtaining a bachelor's degree. Two years later, I graduated from Northrop Institute of Technology in Inglewood, California, with a degree in Aircraft Maintenance Engineering. I was hired back at Pratt into the JT9D experimental engineering test program, where I met my future wife, Brenda.

During this time, I qualified for my private pilot's license and also bought a 1946 Piper Cub. It needed to be rebuilt, and I had the training to do it. Heck, it was like building a model airplane, which I had done so many years ago. Brenda helped me rib-stitch the wings. To do this, a needle about a foot long is punched through the fabric on the top side of the wing and through the bottom side. A knot is then made and the needle advanced back to the top side. As the needle penetrates the taught fabric, it makes a 'pop' sound. This procedure is repeated hundreds of times during this operation. On one occasion, Brenda 'popped' the needle through to my side, and I yelled, "Ow, you got me in the eye!" Of course, she freaked out and I just laughed it off. Not a good way to impress your fiancé.

I modified the wings by cutting off seven feet of the wingspan using a Reed-clipped wing conversion. This made the Cub more aerobatic. I loved to do loops, wingovers, rolls, and spins. Some people don't like the feeling of being upside down or spinning. They get disoriented. I loved it, and it never bothered me. In fact, I savored it. This brings to mind a Confucius saying, 'pilot who fly upside down soon have crack up.' I was young and adventurous, so I never had the thought that flying like this could be dangerous or end in an accident.

Years later, after marrying Brenda, purchasing our first house, and having our first baby, I was flying fewer hours. The rule of thumb was you should fly at least fifty hours a year to stay somewhat proficient. I was not. Between work and family, there was no time to get to the airfield. One winter, I was flying with a fellow engineer, Russ Groff, out of Brainard Airport in Hartford, Connecticut. Because Russ had some flying experience, I sat in the front seat of my tandem-seating Cub with him in the rear seat or 'pilot in command' position. During the flight, fuel started leaking from the twelve-gallon gas tank which is located above the knees of the front seated pilot. With fuel leaking into the cockpit, I instructed Russ to head back to the airport as quickly as possible while I took off my gloves and used them to try to stem the flow of gas. We could turn into a fireball at any moment. This was not a good situation. As luck would have it, we made it back to the airfield without incident and lived to tell about it. The fuel tank was replaced.

A senior engineer, Bill Staley, wanted to get some time in the Cub. So I flew up to Skylark Airport in East Windsor, Connecticut, early one Saturday morning, to pick him up. We flew over to Simsbury Airport for a touch-and-go. Upon climb out, the engine coughed one time, and I thought that was strange, but we continued to fly around the Connecticut foothills for a while longer. After landing back at Skylark, I wanted to fuel up the Cub but the airport was out of gas. I still had a quarter tank remaining, so I figured that would be enough to get me back to Hartford. For some reason, I decided to do a stunt on takeoff. After liftoff, I held the plane down to build up speed and then pulled back to do a performance climb. At the top of the climb, about 200 feet of altitude, the engine coughed and sputtered. I immediately lowered the nose, and the engine resumed running. I tried to make a gentle turn back to the airfield, but the engine sputtered again. Straight and level was my only option while I looked for a place to set the Cub down. As I approached an open field, a sod farm, the engine finally quit. I shoved the nose down to keep from stalling, but the trees at the edge of the field were coming up fast. One more burst of power from the engine gave me enough airspeed to pull up and over the trees and then make a soft landing on the field. The training I had in emergency landings and aerobatics really paid off. Keep the airplane flying, and don't stall it. I turned off the ignition, climbed out of the airplane, and started to walk towards the nearest road. I got maybe a hundred feet from the airplane, and the reality of what had just happened started to set in. My knees weakened and almost buckled under me. The adrenaline was wearing off. I could have just been killed.

The Cub was eventually gassed up, inspected and flown out of the field and back to Skylark by an experienced agricultural pilot. With the responsibilities of a home and a young family, I had tempted fate too many times, and it was at this point that I decided to back away from flying for a while. There would be more flying in my future. The Cub was sold to a local pilot. It then found another owner in North Carolina and currently is with an owner in Ohio. I still have November six five seven Mike (N657M) in my heart and soul.

My 1946 Piper J3C65 clipped wing Cub that I rebuilt in 1967. The picture was taken by Ed Granville at a private airstrip that I flew into in Somers, Connecticut. Ed was one of the Granville Brothers that built the GeeBee racer that won the 1932 Thompson Trophy race.

STOLEN

Shortly after Brenda and I first met, she bought a brand new 1968 Firebird. It was a nice car with a powerful 350 cubic-inch engine. I lavished her with the gift of a few eight-track tapes for her console player, which was factory-installed. I was obviously trying to get some 'points' for the effort. Somewhere around the time we were married in April of 1969, we went to visit a friend in Hartford Hospital. We parked the Firebird in the parking garage across the street from the hospital. Later, when we came out to retrieve the car, we realized that someone had just broken into it and stolen the tape player. Their tools were still on the front seat! They were somewhere nearby and probably watching us. We locked up the car again and went to the entrance of the garage to call the police. While we were waiting for the police, we monitored every vehicle leaving the garage to see if we could spot any suspicious characters, which we did not. The police came and took the report, but refused to go to our car or look for any thieves who we felt might still be in the garage. After the report was completed and the police left, we returned to the car to go home. The Firebird had been broken into again to retrieve tools!! Bastards! Wish I had my gun with me.

We replaced the tape player with a new after-market one. For the first year of our marriage, we lived in a first-floor rental apartment in East Hartford, Connecticut. The Firebird was parked just a few feet from our bedroom window behind our unit. One morning, as we were heading to work, we noticed that the Firebird had been broken into again along with other cars in the parking lot. And, wouldn't you know it, the tape player had been stolen again! Man, you can't have anything nice! Bastards! Still wish I had my gun with me!

Some years later, our BMX van, which we traveled all over the country with was getting tired. The engine was making a slight knocking sound in the lower end. It more than likely was worn crankshaft bearings. We found a mechanic who could replace the bearings but would not guarantee the results. It was cheaper than rebuilding or replacing the engine, so we hired him to do the job. The repair lasted for a while but then started to make noise again. One evening, we decided to take the van up to Riverside Amusement Park and Racetrack in Agawam, Massachusetts to watch the demolition car derby and modified car racing. My father-in-law, Joe, accompanied the kids and me. As we parked the van in the big parking lot, I got my coordinates from the aisle signs so we could locate the van after the races. At the start of the derby, the announcer mentioned that someone had left their parking lights on in their vehicle. It wasn't our vehicle that was announced but I was certain that we may have left ours on as well. I excused myself and went out to the parking lot to check. I used the aisle sign coordinates to locate our van, but there was an empty spot in that location. The realization quickly set in that our van had been stolen. A slow, evil smile crept over my face, knowing that the engine in our vehicle had seen better days and was on its way out. That problem may have just been solved. I went back to the track, gathered up the gang, and reported the incident to park security folks. We found out that two other vehicles had also been stolen out of the same parking lot that night. It must have been a coordinated gang effort. I called Brenda for a ride home.

It was probably two or three days later that we got a call from the Agawam police saying that they found our van in an isolated area, and it was towed to a recovery yard nearby. We went to inspect the vehicle and it was trashed. The thieves had gotten in by prying the sunroof open. The custom wheels were gone, and it was sitting on blocks. Our custom BMX license plate was gone. The custom reclining seats were gone, and every window or sheet metal panel was either smashed or dented. There would be no recovery of this vehicle. It was totaled. Insurance paid off a very generous sum and we went looking for a new car. I secretly wished I could have thanked whoever stole the van. They saved us from replacing a very expensive engine. That slow, evil smile crept over my face again. Good timing!

HOUSES

My wife, Brenda, and I have been fortunate. We started life together by renting an inexpensive apartment in East Hartford, Connecticut. It was in a housing development near where we worked at Pratt & Whitney. Because of federal loan guarantees, the owner could only charge so much for rent. I think we were paying around $115 per month when coworkers were paying three times that amount in the newest apartment complexes nearby. However, this housing was not without problems; we had an eight-track tape unit stolen from Brenda's nearly new 1968 Pontiac Firebird, and the coin-operated washer and dryer in the basement had been broken into multiple times. It wasn't long before we paid off my student loans and saved enough money for a down payment on a house. After just over a year in the apartment, we started looking to purchase a place of our own.

Our search brought us to a new development in Coventry, Connecticut. The houses in this development were generally ranches, raised ranches, or colonials. We spotted a new Tudor-style raised ranch that was being constructed on Fieldstone Lane. It was being used for a model home. We negotiated a price of $27,200. Additionally, we got a discount for painting the interior and rear deck. We put $10,000 down and closed on our first house. After moving in, some people walked in on us, thinking that it was still a model home! They were embarrassed but we thought it was funny. We still talk about that incident to this day.

We were in the Coventry house for seven years and started our young family there. Kimberly and Brett started life in this house. We wanted to move to Manchester, Connecticut, because it was closer to work and all of the kids' activities were centered there. We spotted a house on Strawberry Lane that was in foreclosure because the builder went bankrupt. We missed buying the house at auction, but ended up purchasing it from the broker who turned a quick profit on the deal. It took me six months of hard work to finish the new house before we could get the certificate of occupancy to move in. In the meantime, we were also preparing our Coventry house for sale. One night, we were lying in bed when we heard a terrible crash downstairs that woke us out of a sound sleep. It sounded and felt like a car or airplane had crashed into the house. It was that loud. I jumped out of bed and went downstairs to investigate. I had no idea what I was going to find. As I made my way into the garage area under our master (primary) bedroom and turned on the light, I spotted one of the garage door springs hanging down and swinging back and forth. Holy shit! If someone had been in the area of that spring failure, it could have killed them. We were lucky that no one had gotten hurt. The next day, I fixed the spring (should have replaced it, but we were trying to save money) by heating and bending the end to recreate the attachment hook. In the future, springs like this would have a cable running through them to prevent a failure of this type from hurting anybody. I'm willing to bet there were lawsuits associated with garage door spring failures. Just saying.

We raised our children in the Manchester house and held on to it for 27 years. I was now in the hot rod car hobby and needed extra garage space. I was looking at ways we could add another garage, but the layout of this colonial house and the lot size would not permit it. About this time, one of the premier builders in town had just purchased a nearby farm and was going to build a new development of custom homes. As the roads and utilities were being put in, I approached Andrew Ansaldi and told him we wanted to be his first customer. We selected what I considered the best lot in the new development. It was on a cul-de-sac at the top of the hill overlooking the Connecticut River valley and the Metacomet Ridge on the horizon. We struck up a deal and selected a house plan which included a third-car garage. We finally closed on 367 Bella Vista Lane after almost a year of construction. We sold our Strawberry Lane house on our own in one weekend but had to rent it back from the new owners for three months until the new house was ready. Pushing Ansaldi to finish our new house, Ansaldi commented, "Well, you sold your old house too soon!" Oh, the trials and tribulations of house ownership. We owned the Bella Vista Lane house for ten years until our transition to Florida, but that is a story for another chapter.

BABIES

After my wife, Brenda, and I got married, we saved our pennies and bought our first house in Coventry, Connecticut. It was a Tudor-style raised ranch. After we moved in, we started to think about starting a family. So, we practiced a lot because practice makes perfect! Right? One day, Brenda announced to me that she was pregnant (or as they say today, WE were pregnant). I was so elated that, without thinking, I ran out of the house and went up and down the street, neighbor to neighbor to announce the good news. Holy shit, that thing down there really works! It was the beginning of making a family together. We were entering the next phase of our lives. Things were getting much more serious now, and my responsibilities were skyrocketing as a new husband, a provider, and a future father. My bachelor years were now in the rear view mirror!

Our first child was a girl who we named Kimberly. I have many fond memories of her as she was growing up into the fine woman that she is today. Christmas is always a nice time of year, especially when you have children. Preparing for our first holiday with our young daughter was special. Kimberly was about eight months old that first year, and I remember we could not get her to go to sleep on Christmas Eve so we could put Santa's gifts under the tree. I looked down the hall into her bedroom, and there she was, standing at the edge of her crib trying to see what was going on. I said to her in a very stern, deep voice, "Santa won't come to visit at our house if you don't go to sleep!" She must have realized the importance of the moment because her reaction was to let go of the side of the crib. Gravity took over as she flopped backward into a prone position. I never heard another peep from her the rest of the night. She was out like a light. And, no, she didn't hit her head when she fell backward!

Kids are funny. They provide entertainment in various forms as they grow up. Some are good and some are not so good. I can see why parents tell their kids, "If you don't behave, I'm going to kill you and make another one!" Our son, Brett, was born when Kimberly was about two years old. We were on a business trip in Florida for a number of months. We tell our son that he was conceived under a palm tree, which is not too far from the truth. Brett was delivered by C-section. I was so nervous about the operation that I called Brenda's mother and told her she had a vasectomy! I never lived that down. Brett has grown into a fine young man and is a great father. We cherish his accomplishments in life.

There would be one more child in the making between Kimberly and Brett, but that was not to be. Complications sadly terminated the pregnancy. It was a very deeply personal moment for us. I'm not sure if everyone believes in clairvoyant mediums, but we have had two experiences with readings from them that were amazing. In both cases, they stated that we had three children. The third one was the pregnancy loss. Both psychics said that the baby would have been a girl. One psychic said the name was Stacy. That was the name we had chosen. They stated that she was watching us from beyond and that one day, we would get to see her again in another life. There was no way that these clairvoyants could have possibly known about this event in our lives. It makes you wonder if there is a higher power in the universe and if God has a plan for all of us and speaks to us through certain gifted people. There are many things that we don't understand in life.

Brenda goes to church regularly. I believe in God but don't attend church except on rare occasions. I tell everyone that I go to Saint Bonifay or Saint Hacienda Hills on Sunday. These are actually golf courses. My intentions are pure. We both believe in prayer, but I don't think it matters whether the prayers are said in a church or at a golf course or in private. They are all being received by our maker. We pray regularly for our children and grandchildren. Lord, hear our prayers!

Brenda always wanted a larger family, but we stopped after the second birth because I didn't want her to risk another C-section operation. It was a compromise. Life goes on.

BROKEN BONES

None of us are going to escape this life without a few broken bones. My first experience with this was when I was ten or eleven years old. We were playing at recess at school. I somehow ended up on the ground, and a friend said, "Here, let me help you up." He extended a hand, and as I was halfway up, he let go. My right leg buckled under me in an awkward fashion, and I immediately felt pain. I toughed it out and got through the rest of the day. I even walked home after school, but the pain kept getting worse. A visit to the doctor and a subsequent X-ray revealed a fracture in my tibia or fibula, I don't remember which. So, into a cast I went, and it would be six weeks of walking with crutches. During the healing process, I took a couple of falls. One occasion happened coming downstairs with the crutches, which got hung up on an upper tread, launching me into mid-air. The railing mitigated an ensuing disaster. Without the crutches, I was hopping around on one foot and tripped over a threshold. I made a nice three-point landing!

Later in life, I was navigating my way to my truck in the driveway on a cold winter day. I stepped on ice that was coming from a dripping rain gutter downspout. My feet went out from under me. I broke the fall with my hands and my feet ended up under the truck. The pain in my wrist warranted a visit to the emergency room where it was confirmed that I had a fracture in one of the bones in my wrist. Years later, I occasionally have pain in that wrist, and it reminds me of the accident that happened all those years ago.

It was my first day of retirement, January 2009. I had just cleared the driveway of snow with the snowblower. I had put a little sand and salt on our sloping driveway so Brenda would have no problem backing down to the cul-de-sac on her way to work. The newspaper had been delivered earlier, and it was lying at the edge of the road. I figured I'd be smart and walk down to the road on the snow-covered lawn so I wouldn't slip. As I stepped on our front sidewalk, my feet went out from under me, and I landed flat on my back. Damn, black ice. The fall hurt, but I got up, told Brenda I was okay and off to work she went.

As the day progressed, I worked on my 1932 Ford hot rod project. Since I had been working 2nd shift at the Pratt & Whitney plant in Middletown, Connecticut at the time of my retirement, I needed to go there to hand in my badge and say my goodbyes to everyone. I drove there, still hurting from the fall, and began my farewell tour at the engine test and engine assembly buildings. On my way out, I handed in my badge to the guard at the entrance of the facility. I have to admit this was a very emotional moment for me. I was ending a grand and illustrious 43-year career at this company where I had met my wife and been involved in some very interesting projects over the years. I shed some tears on my way home.

After a couple of drinks to numb my hurting back, I went off to bed. Early the next morning, I got up to take a whiz. On my way back to bed, I heard something snap in my back and the pain drove me to my knees. Brenda was concerned but I told her to just go to work. I'd be okay. As the day wore on, the pain got worse. I called Brenda at work and asked for her advice as to what to do. I just needed something for pain relief. She said, "The doctor won't prescribe anything for you unless he sees you." So, we called our PCP and made an appointment for later that afternoon. No ambulance for me, so Brenda came home to drive me to the doctor. I couldn't even get into her car because of the pain, so I opted for my truck which had a step bar and a handle to assist me into the front seat. With my shirt off, the doctor pointed to the throbbing location in my back and said to Brenda, "He broke at least three ribs! You don't even have to go to the hospital or get an X-ray because they will tell you the same thing."

Six weeks of sitting and sleeping in my computer chair was all I could do. "Don't let the kids or grandkids come over because if I catch a cold from them and have to cough, I'm gonna die!"

Hopefully, there will be no more broken bones in my future. That shit hurts!!

SHOOTING

I've been into shooting since I was a little boy. My dad was a hunter and taught my sister and me how to shoot a rifle, shotgun, and handgun safely at a young age. When I was 12 years old, my birthday present was a J C Higgins bolt action 22 caliber rifle with a five-shot magazine and a four-power optical scope. I never disappointed my parents and used that gun safely all my life. I still have it and shoot it occasionally in my old age. I walked to the downtown Clinton, Massachusetts, armory with it in my hand many times to shoot in the basement range. I never got stopped by the police or turned in by an informer while doing this. Back in those days, 1956, it was considered no big deal. Carrying on the tradition, I taught both of my kids to shoot. My wife, Brenda, was brought up in the city, had no guns in the house, and didn't learn to shoot until she met me. She now has her own handgun and a pistol permit to carry concealed. That's my kind of woman!

I started shooting archery with my son Brett when he was a

teenager. We shot at Hall's Arrow in Manchester, Connecticut, and at an outdoor range in Tolland. The Hall brothers and sisters competed nationally and in the Olympics, so they were a good resource to learn from. One weekend we attended an open house at the indoor range. Brett won a really nice compound bow that was too big for him at the time, so I eventually bought it from him. At the open house, some guy was selling raffle tickets. I declined the offer to purchase from him. Later, a hot girl came around selling the same tickets. As she approached me, Brett leaned over to his buddy and said, "I bet he'll buy them now!" He was right. I bought the tickets! Smart ass kid! I went on to win a gold medal in the Nutmeg Games with that compound bow. These games were the equivalent of the state Olympics.

Eventually, I switched over to pistol shooting. We had an indoor range behind our house in one of the buildings at the old Nike missile base. I joined one of the teams and started to compete statewide. I got pretty good at it. A perfect score is 300. I shot in the 280s, so I felt pretty good about myself. At some point in time, I was approached by members to run for Vice President of the club. I ended up winning the election, served as VP for two years, and President for two years. It was a lot of work and it was political at times, but I survived and did some good things for the club.

Two of my team members, Wally and Fran, were teaching pistol permit courses at the club and urged me to join them. So, I took the required NRA instructor course, obtained my credentials, and began teaching once a week. It was fun, and I met a lot of interesting people. Some were from rough areas of Hartford and just wanted to protect themselves. One student had been shot and robbed and vowed to never let that happen again. One weekend, we held a course for a dozen doctors. One of their fellow doctor's homes had been broken into resulting in the killing of the wife and daughter. They wanted to protect themselves going forward. The doctors felt they were targets in their affluent neighborhoods. I've taught schoolteachers, lady judges, stuntmen, and even a former Czechoslovakian sniper. He knew how to 'squeeze' a trigger properly, which is probably the #1 secret to accurately shooting a pistol or rifle.

During one classroom session, Wally was teaching a lesson on trigger squeeze. We all did this segment of the class with a 45 Colt pistol that was secretly loaded with a primer-only cartridge in the chamber. Wally didn't have time to prepare the proper dummy round which sounded like a cap pistol going off, so he used a commercially available blank cartridge. Blank cartridges have powder in them and a wad to hold the powder in place. When fired, it is as loud as a live round and the wad comes out of the gun like a bullet. Wally proceeded to blow a training chart off the wall to the surprise of the class and Fran and me in the office! We told the students to take a five-minute break so we could clean up the mess. Good thing nobody got hurt, and there were no resulting lawsuits.

I still teach to this day and have taught many of our neighbors here in Florida. I estimate I have taught over 1,000 students in the 30 years I have been a certified NRA pistol instructor. One memorable moment that sticks in my mind is the time I had a couple come over to the house for some discussion on guns and marksmanship training. The lady handed me her semi-automatic 22-caliber target pistol. The first thing I always do when handling a gun is to make sure it is "safe." I teach all of my students this because shooting is all about safety. I removed the magazine first which is the source of ammunition. I slid back (racked) the slide, and to my amazement, a live cartridge was ejected! This lady had handed me a loaded gun! The safety was off, and the gun was cocked. If I had just touched the trigger, the gun would have fired, and really bad things could have been the result. ALWAYS MAKE YOUR GUN SAFE!

Our son is a police officer and uses all the skills he learned from me and from his police training. He was a range officer at the police department for a number of years, training and qualifying all of the other officers. My daughter is a schoolteacher and shoots all the time. She is currently working for Cabela's selling... you guessed it... guns. She also wants to obtain her NRA pistol instructor rating. My kids are both better shots than me. Apparently, the apple doesn't fall too far from the tree. I am a firm believer in the 2nd amendment. That's the one that protects all the other amendments.

BMX

BMX stands for bicycle motocross racing. It was a fairly new sport in the early 1980s and consisted of bicycle racing on a clay dirt track with jumps, turns and straightaways. The race would start, usually on a hill, with a starting gate. As many as six or eight racers lined up with their front wheels touching the gate. A cadence was called out by the starter. "Riders ready? Watch the gate! Beep, beep, beep," and the gate dropped for the start of the race.

A local bicycle shop petitioned the town of Manchester, Connecticut, to use a patch of land at the old Nike missile base to build a racetrack for the new sport. This land was used for various recreational activities over the years, including a ski slope, hiking trails, a baseball field, various buildings for daycare, a dance studio, and even a shooting range. After approval by the town, work began by bringing in truckloads of clay and creating a track with berms, turns, jumps of various shapes (tabletop, double, single), and a straightaway to a finish line. The sport was sanctioned by a national BMX association which spelled out the rules for local and national races.

Our son, Brett, who was about five years old at the time, took an interest in the sport. We decided to give it a try, so I took his old 20" wheeled bike and removed the fenders. We registered with the National Association and obtained his novice identification number. The number was affixed to a plastic license plate and mounted at the front of his handlebars. A helmet was also required which we purchased. The races were arranged by age and class. Brett soon raced for the first time and did quite well on his old bike. Depending on the number of racers in a class, races (called motos) were conducted and the top four in each moto advanced to the main or final race to determine a winner.

It wasn't long before Brett started getting better and better. To be more competitive, we bought him a new racing bicycle. He started to win races. It was about this time that there was enough interest in the sport that they started girls' classes. Our daughter, Kimberly, expressed an interest in competing. I took her old pink girl's bike, removed the fenders, sanded it down, and painted it black. She was registered as a novice with the association and received her number to display on the front of her bike. She did pretty well on that old bicycle and it wasn't long before we upgraded her to a new racing bike also.

Before long, another track opened in South Windsor, and we began racing there as well. Both Brett and Kimberly finally advanced to the expert class as the trophies started rolling in. A national race was coming up in Syracuse, New York, and we decided as a team to give it a try. The kids did quite well against stiff competition and Kimberly ended up with a 2nd or 3rd place trophy for her efforts. This was getting serious now. Since the start of a race was most important, I built a starting gate at home for practice. Getting the 'hole shot' was the goal. The kids also trained doing 'burnouts' pedaling uphill as fast as they could for as long as they could to build up leg muscles.

Brenda and I also raced occasionally with adults on larger 24" cruiser-class bikes. We had fun, but we were not as competitive as our children. One fond memory I have is my crashing over the starting gate when it didn't drop at the start of a race. Eight adults, including me, were catapulted head-first onto the pavement at the same time. It must have been a scary sight for spectators. A collective groan from the crowd confirmed the theory. We all got up, brushed ourselves off, and went back to racing.

We raced locally and nationally for at least five years. We traveled all over the country with our van (BMX license plate) and matching custom trailer. We even flew to Florida for a national race in Homestead, and drove to Montgomery, Alabama, for a Christmas week race. We competed in a national race in Nashville, Tennessee. That year, 1984, both kids were state champions in their respective age groups in Massachusetts, Connecticut, and Rhode Island. What an accomplishment! Both kids had accumulated enough national points to compete in the Grand National race in Louisville, Kentucky. Brett finished well with a 15th-place national ranking in his very competitive age group. Kimberly needed to come in 4th place or better in her final race to become the national champion. She did by edging out a big California girl at the finish line!

I have never been a champion at anything in my life, either local, state, or national, so I am proud of Kim's and Brett's accomplishments. Of course, it was a team effort. I'm grateful for the memories.

A picture of Kimberly and Brett with some of their trophies that they won racing Bicycle Motocross. They were both ranked #1 in their age groups in Massachusetts, Connecticut, and Rhode Island in 1984. Kim was also ranked National #1 that year and Brett was ranked National #14.

Hot Rods

It started from an early age. I have always liked mechanical things and making stuff with my hands. I was never much into electronics. I absorbed what I had to in college to get by, but I never would have become an electrical engineer or computer geek. I knew people who built their own radios, televisions, and computers. Not me. Give me airplanes, tractors, and cars and I'd be a happy camper. My introduction to cars was at an amusement park not too far from our home in central Massachusetts. I was probably around eight years old and met the height requirement for a ride, which allowed the solo driver to steer a Model T replica car around a course lined with sideboards so you couldn't go off the track. I drove the course without hitting any of the sideboards. I was pretty proud of myself.

The next experience driving anything was when I was about ten years old. Our English Setter family dog, Lady Pepper, was getting on in years and having problems just doing basic functions. I had this dog as a friend I could talk to and play with since I was little. My dad took her to the vet one day with me in tow. I still remember comforting Pepper while she sat shivering on a stainless-steel table. After the vet examined her, he prepared a syringe, walked back to the table, and injected her. I had no idea what was about to happen. Lady Pepper looked at me, started to lose her bodily functions, slumped on the cold table, and died right in front of me. When I came to the realization of what had happened, I cried. I was devastated that the vet and my dad would allow a young kid to witness something like this. I can remember the event like it was yesterday. To soften the blow, we went for a ride in the car before we went home. My dad let me sit on his lap and steer the car for a while to get my mind off of Lady Pepper. It didn't really help, but I do remember the experience of steering a real car for the first time.

As I approached my teens, I got a seasonal job at an apple orchard in the town of Bolton, Massachusetts. I graduated from picking dropped apples off the ground for the cider mill to picking from the trees to driving some of the farm machinery. It wasn't long before I was driving tractors, bulldozers, and trucks. I was in my element. Within days after turning 16 and getting my license, I bought my first car. It was a 1950 Pontiac. My dad had traded it in for a new car from a local Dodge dealer. The dealer sold it to me for $50. It wasn't long before I started customizing it like most kids did back in the day. A glass-packed muffler to get that loud, mellow exhaust sound. Nose and decking the hood and trunk by removing chrome and filling the holes. Modifying the stance of the car and lowering the nose by heating the front coil springs. Installing a LaSalle transmission with a floor stick shift. A new paint job was done in the driveway. I thought I was a pretty hot shit at the time and the girls liked it, too. 'Nuff said. I kept this car until I started going to college in Boston. I think I sold the Pontiac for $50 to another kid in town. It owed me nothing.

Me and my sister with my first "hot rod." It was a 1950 Pontiac that I bought for $50. I modified the exhaust system with a glass pack muffler, stripped chrome off of the hood and trunk (called nosing and decking), spray painted it in the driveway, lowered the front suspension, and installed a LasSalle transmission with a floor shift.

Over the years, I had many cars like a Chevy Corvair, a new 1965 Ford Mustang and a 1960 Corvette. It wasn't until after getting married and starting a family that I got bitten by the hot rod bug again. I found a 1937 Ford Tudor slant-back sedan for sale. It was in a barn in Marlboro, Connecticut. I purchased it for $500 and had it trailered to our house by a friend. When Brenda, my wife, saw it, she exclaimed, "You paid how much for that piece of junk?" Are you kidding me? Just because it had no engine or transmission, was missing the seats, was rusted, needed new windows and a paint job? I thought it was a thing of beauty and saw the potential in it. Fast forward a year later and the car was done. An engine and transmission from a donor car, some bodywork, a driveway paint job, and a whole lot of other things, and I had a new hot rod. I have other memories of building this car that I could share like the steering column being, quite literally, dug up from the ground by a friend, wiring the car from scratch with scrapped wire from work, and trading a favorite gun for help with the donor car. The list goes on and on, but I finally sold the car to a fellow in New Jersey for $5,000. I made a little money on the sale and got a great deal of enjoyment from building this car.

My 1937 Ford Tudor Sedan shown with Larry Krizan's 1936 ford Cabriolet. I spent a year rebuilding the '37, installing a drive train from a 1967 Ford station wagon, and painting it in the driveway. I found this car in a barn and bought it for $500. My wife, Brenda, bragged that she left rubber (peeled out) with it! After enjoying the car for a few years, I sold it to a guy in New Jersey for $5000.

I bought a 1932 Ford rumble seat coupe on a whim. It was an original car that I planned to make into a hot rod someday. Our son tripped and fell out of the rumble seat in the garage one day and hit his head on the floor. A trip to the hospital emergency room determined that he would be fine. He must have a hard head like his dad. My dad used to say, "Good thing you hit your head otherwise, you might have hurt yourself!" Dear old Dad had a saying for every occasion. The '32 Ford was sold to a couple for a little more than I paid for it. I had decided I didn't need another car project at that time. What I did need, however, was a hot rod. I found a 1930 Ford rumble seat roadster in California that was for sale. The car had been built by Jim Garcia and was now owned by Richard Wickert. We settled on a price of $25,000, and I had it transported to Connecticut. The car had a history of being displayed at the L.A. Roadster show in Pomona for years. It was painted a bright Porsche Indian red. It looked like a jewel coming off the enclosed trailer. I ended up owning this car for 20 years. I made some changes to it, like adding rear bumpers, installing rumble seat cushions, rebuilding the headers and exhaust system, and installing a chopped convertible top. When it was time to move on, I sold the car through Gateway Classic Cars in Orlando for $43,000. The car owed me nothing.

My 1930 Ford rumble seat roadster. Built by Jim Garcia and bought from Richard Wickert in California for $25,000. I rebuilt the entire exhaust system, installed the chopped convertible top, upholstered the rumble seat, and installed rear bumpers with step pads. I enjoyed this car for 20 years and recently sold it for $43,000. Not bad for a Model A car that sold for $385 new!

While I owned the roadster, I also started building a 1932 Ford coupe. What's better than having a hot rod? Having two hot rods, of course! This car turned out to be an eight-year project. It was the first and only car I ever chopped, which was a favorite modification to race cars to lower their overall height, lessen wind resistance, and go faster. I have many stories to tell about this car, and it could take a whole book to describe them. In fact, I did write a book about this car that you can read about in *The Deuce Coupe that Stole My Heart*. It's no secret that I still love old cars and hot rods to this day. I've still got "the bug."

My 1932 Ford 5 Window Coupe. An original car found in the woods of Minnesota. I bought this car from a shop in Nebraska for $17,000 and spent 8 years building it. Most of the effort was spent on the body and chopped roof. When it was finished, I took it to several national shows and countless cruise nights, It was featured in the March 2011 issue of Street Rodder magazine. I, personally, have $50,000 invested in this car but it is worth much more than that. I've been told by my family that I cannot sell the '32. It will remain in the family.

Magazine

I built my 1932 Ford hot rod from scratch. Little did I know it was going to be an eight-year project. Originally, the car was found abandoned in the woods of Minnesota by a couple of game wardens. It was rescued from there and eventually made its way to a hot rod shop in Grand Island, Nebraska. This shop put a new frame under it and did some shoddy workmanship on the body to make it presentable enough to sell. Along comes Dick Stoebel who found the car by internet search. Even though the internet was still in its infancy, it would be the way that I would also purchase four or five of our family cars over the coming years. A deal was struck to purchase the '32 and have it transported to Connecticut. The purchase price was in the neighborhood of $17,000. When my wife Brenda saw it for the first time, I got the same reaction from her that I did on a previous purchase of a 1937 Ford. "You paid how much for this piece of junk?" I could see that it had 'good bones' even though it was pretty much 'bare bones' with no engine, no transmission, no seats, no instruments, no windows, no... Well, let's just leave it at that. It became really clear that this car would need a lot of attention to get it back into road-worthy condition.

After beginning to restore this original 'Henry' steel car, we decided to move to a new house nearby that was being built for us. The new house was going to have a third-car garage which would become my workshop. After moving, work resumed on the '32. Most of the time-consuming work was in the sheet metal. The bottom ten inches of the body was basically rust. An attempt by the Nebraska folks to do some body work was poorly done so I ended up cutting it all out and starting over. Patch panels were not available for some areas, so I hand fabricated those panels where required. To me, it's very therapeutic working with sheet metal. Some of the art of welding and fabrication was learned during aviation mechanic training. Some was learned by research and trial and error... lots of errors! At some point in the build, I retired from Pratt & Whitney after a 43-year career. Now I had the best of both worlds. I could work on my project car just about every day while my wife, Brenda, was still working. UPS and FedEx trucks delivered parts frequently. It was like a continuous flow of Christmas presents arriving daily.

As the days, weeks, and years passed by, and with the help of friends, my project car was ready to leave the nest. First, it was off to the body shop in Granby, Connecticut, then to the paint shop in Windsor Locks, then on to the glass shop in Ellington, and finally to the upholstery guy in Vernon. I registered the car without ever going to the Motor Vehicle Department (MVD). Getting a fenderless Hiboy hot rod registered at the MVD would be impossible, so the VIN check was done by a hot rod-friendly shop in Coventry for $20. MY32 vintage Connecticut license plate was verified at the more friendly MVD in Willimantic, and voila, I could now legally drive the car on the street. There is no annual emissions check for cars that are 25 or more years old, so that ordeal could be avoided as well. Let me mention again: this is a fenderless hot rod. Cops are generally friendly to hot rodders as long as you didn't get caught speeding or doing burnouts. I tell people who are not car savvy that Ford built a standard and a deluxe version of the 1932 coupe. The cheaper standard version came without fenders! I actually got some people to believe this.

Because the car was freshly built, I took it to national shows all over the northeast. I also contacted the editor of *Street Rodder Magazine*, Brian Brennan, to see if he might be interested in featuring my car. He responded, asking for some photos, which I immediately sent to him. He liked what he saw, so he assigned Chuck Vranas to shoot the pictures and write the article. Chuck spent the afternoon with me at my garage and then at the old Nike missile base nearby to take photos. It was a nice experience, and the feature article hit the newsstands in the March 2011 issue. This, to me, was like hitting the lottery, having my car featured in a national magazine. It made all the hard work worthwhile, but now it was depressing to see the UPS and FedEx delivery trucks come into our neighborhood, circle the cul-de-sac in front of our house, and then leave without stopping. Maybe it was time for another project!

Cops

Growing up and from a young age, I had the highest respect for police officers. Their authority came without question. The rule of law is necessary to maintain a civil society. Today is another story altogether. Woke is the term now used to spread awareness of racial injustice and, for some reason, it has evolved into calls for defunding police and other extreme measures that will surely lead to disorder and anarchy. We now see disrespect for authority, which personally, scares the hell out of me. That is why I 'keep my powder dry.' We could actually have another civil war.

When our son, Brett, was young, he was the kid who always stuck up for others being bullied. He recognized that bullying was not acceptable from an early age. As he got a little older, he must have rubbed one or more of the bullies the wrong way because he suffered repercussions. One incident occurred overnight as our family Buick was parked in front of the house. We awoke to find one of the windows shot out. Police were called to investigate but I don't think anything ever came of it. Not too long after, the windows were smashed on Brett's Ford Bronco parked at the curb. A rock was thrown so hard that it went right through the rear window and hit the front windshield. I'm thinking that our son must have pissed off someone again. Just a wild guess. We had to have both of the windows replaced. Thank God for glass coverage with our insurance company. We cautioned Brett to be careful out there. The enemies he was making could be his demise.

One evening, the doorbell rang. I answered the door to find a young punk asking to have our son step outside. I spotted two more lurking around the corner. They had bad intentions. I let Brett know and immediately retrieved my loaded 45 Colt pistol. While I was getting my gun, one of the bad boys who was trained as a golden glove boxer got ready to take a swing at Brett. Our son knew how to protect himself with Jiu-Jitsu and countered with a punch to the stomach. They both landed on the front sidewalk and lawn. At that moment, I swung the front screen door open and pointed the 45 at them. When the punks saw the gun, they scrambled to get back to their car. I chased them and yelled, "Don't ever f**k with my family or you'll end up dead!" After stalling the car a couple of times, they finally sped away. The next morning, the punks showed up at a neighbor's house when our son was picking up his friends. Their father came out with a shotgun and scared them off again. That was the last we saw of them. They got the message. As it turns out, these dudes were from a bad 'hood' in Hartford. They were street fighters and known to possess homemade and illegal firearms. This was the dark side of programs that relocated inner-city families to the suburbs. Our town of Manchester was once known as

"The City of Village Charm." It's no longer charming, and it is one of the reasons we sold our house there and retired to Florida.

Brett eventually went off to college at Central Connecticut State University. He was interested in sports training. He was athletic right from the start. Skateboarding, hockey, bicycle motocross (BMX) racing, dirt bikes. He did it all very well. He was state champion in Massachusetts, Connecticut, and Rhode Island BMX one year and was ranked 15th nationally. Great accomplishments. But, after a year at Central, he became more interested in criminal justice and switched to Manchester Community College. This is the kid who "borrowed" his sister's Camaro one night and went joyriding with his friends. He didn't even have his license yet. After a close call with the police at a 7-11 store, he made his way home and parked the car. The next morning, our daughter noticed that her car was parked in a slightly different location than she had left it, so our suspicions were raised. We got the full story after an interrogation. And this kid wants to be a cop? After graduating from MCC, Brett attended the University of New Haven, still concentrating on criminal justice. This was the school associated with Henry Lee, the renowned forensic scientist who was involved with the O. J. Simpson trial and the investigation into the assassination of John F. Kennedy. Brett went on to graduate with his Bachelor of Science degree from this school.

While looking for employment, Brett applied to a number of police departments. Our town of Manchester was one of them. He was rejected because he failed to state on his application that he had been arrested. He had been detained years earlier with a bunch of other kids who were hanging out on private property at the edge of town. The police took their names, but Brett never knew he had been "arrested."

His application to the Stamford, Connecticut police department was accepted. They chose 12 of 1,200 applicants to enter into their police academy, and Brett was one of them. He competed with military veterans who had an advantage because of their service. After completing training, he graduated and became a full-fledged police officer. During his career, he had many assignments. Eventually, he qualified for the marine division and obtained his captain's credentials. He loved boating and fishing, so this was right up his alley. He then moved on to the Special Response Team (SRT), previously known as SWAT. He was a founding member of SRT and did a stint with the narcotics squad as well. Narcotics enforcement was intense, and after seven years he had had enough of that. It was wearing him down, and he had no family life with constant contact from 'informants.' It was time to move on. About this time, he got his master's degree and was promoted to sergeant. I had the distinct privilege of pinning his award on him at the ceremony. Still an SRT operative and trained as a sniper, he took over the duties of chief range officer involved in the training and qualifying of other officers. He was schooled as an armorer for the type of guns his officers were carrying at the time. This was a huge responsibility because if a firearm he worked on was involved in an incident, he could be held liable for damages. And, to top it all off, the governor of Connecticut signed into law a bill that rescinded an officer's right to immunity. This meant that a civil or criminal lawsuit could be filed against an officer by a victim or family of a victim, which could result in the loss of his home and personal savings. Not a good situation for a proactive police officer.

After 12 years as an SRT operative and the ill effects of on-the-job injuries, Brett finally decided to resign from the team. He was presented with a beautiful plaque by the team for his service. We have a copy of that award prominently displayed at our home in Florida. Brett moved to a less demanding post within the department and, as of this writing, has a few more years to go before he can take advantage of a well-earned retirement. As 30 years of service approaches, Brett, his beautiful wife Maria, and their two teenage boys have their sights set on the 142-acre retirement property just purchased in West Virginia. We've been there. It's beautiful country.

God bless all police officers who keep us safe, and God bless America.

Our son, Brett, is an officer in the Stamford, Connecticut police force. He was very active in the narcotics squad for 7 years and a founding member of the Special Response Team (SRT) for 13 years. This award was given to him when he left the team because of on-the-job injuries. He is looking forward to retirement in a few years after having a very proactive career. God bless our men in blue.

TRAINS

I've always liked trains. I think it's the mechanical workings that draw me in. My exposure to them pretty much started with a train I received for Christmas as a young boy. I was probably around ten years old when my father built a ping pong table in the basement. It was for my sister and me to enjoy. We actually did play ping pong on it for a while. On Christmas morning, after all our presents were opened in the living room around the tree, I was directed to the basement. To my surprise, my dad had converted the table from a paddle game to a model railroad complete with tracks, a tunnel, switches, a steam locomotive, railroad cars, and a caboose! He must have worked all night on it. A real thrill for a young boy. In the coming days and years, I spent many hours playing with the train set, adding accessories such as houses, cars, trees, and even a mail pickup station. My dad had chosen an American Flyer set because of the two-rail system which he felt was more realistic than the three-rail Lionel sets. I couldn't agree more.

Our house in Clinton, Massachusetts was located at the edge of town near the town of Bolton. In fact, our property was half in Clinton and half in Bolton. Our garage was actually in the neighboring town and we paid taxes in both of those towns. A boyhood friend, Terry Linsteadt, lived in Bolton on the other side of the tracks. A railroad passed between our two houses. A few times a week, the train came chugging along to deliver coal, bulk animal feed, and supplies to the nearby town center. You could hear it coming by putting your ear to the rail. Sometimes, we placed a penny on the track and the train pressed it into a flat piece of metal. Just something that kids used to do in the old days. My dad had a funny little parable about a cat crossing the rails as a train was approaching. The cat was slow in crossing and lost a piece of his tail. When he stuck his head back over the rail to look at the severed tail, he lost his head. The moral of the story was, "Don't lose your head over a piece of tail!" The fable had more meaning as I got older and is still relevant to this day!

Because my friend Terry was a railroad buff, he would stand near the railroad crossing as the engineer was delivering coal cars and animal feed boxcars to the parallel rail siding nearby. The engineer sometimes stopped the big diesel-powered locomotive and invited us aboard. I don't know if that was a legal thing for him to do, and I'm sure it was a huge liability issue, but in the old days, they didn't worry too much about things like that. We were onboard the locomotive in the control compartment during the entire switching and delivery process. We were even allowed to work the controls under the supervision of the engineer. Quite a thrill for a young boy. Today, with litigation and lawsuits trying to win millions of dollars in settlements for clients, a ride like this is surely a thing of the past. Give me "the good old days," thank you very much! Times sure have changed, and not for the better, I'm afraid.

My next encounter with trains was years later when we took our five-year-old granddaughter, Tuesday, to Essex, Connecticut. They had an old steam locomotive that took us for a scenic ride north, along the Connecticut River. We stopped at a park near a boat dock, where we transferred to a large river boat. Our granddaughter exclaimed, "I've been to this park before!" She was right. As an infant, she had gone to a picnic at the park and remembered every detail of it. Amazing observation from a youngster. We boarded the boat for a short tour up the river to Gillette Castle and the Goodspeed Opera House. Then, it was back to the train for the return to Essex. These old steam trains are very nostalgic and fun to ride on, but I am told neighbors along the tracks aren't big fans of them because they spew all kinds of coal ash dust into the air. I guess it's like building your house next to an airport and then complaining about the noise. You can't please everyone and it's not a perfect world.

On a business trip to Zurich, Switzerland I had the pleasure of riding the rail system to Lucerne. We took a train from the airport to the main terminal in Zurich. The terminal looks like you've gone back in time. To me, it looked like it probably did back in the early 1900s. The conductors operate the trains on a very precise schedule. At the exact minute, our train pulled out of the station on its way to Lucerne. If you've never been to Zurich or Lucerne, you would be in for a treat. Everything is so clean and pristine along the tracks and in the cities, unlike the trash you see everywhere in the United States. We even encountered a little old lady walking through the park with her cane. As she approached a trash can with some litter on the ground near it, she stopped, bent over, picked up the trash, and deposited it in the can. Cleanliness is almost an obsession with the Swiss people. We could learn a lot from them. Anyhow, we took the return train from Lucerne back to Zurich and from Zurich back to the airport. What a memorable experience that was riding the rails in Switzerland.

It would be another couple of decades before we would take a train ride again. As snowbirds, we seasonally drove from Connecticut to Florida and back again. Each year, the trip seemed to get longer. There is so much traffic, especially when people are heading south in the fall and north in the spring, and they are all traveling at a high rate of speed. Add many more trucks to the mix ever since COVID-19 struck in early 2020 and it is dangerous and stressful driving the long trek along the east coast. At some point, we decided to try the Amtrack Auto Train that runs from Lorton, Virginia to Sanford, Florida. We drove from Connecticut down to Lorton and got our car loaded onto one of the boxcars made specifically to hold ten vehicles each on two levels. With thirty boxcars, they can transport up to 300 automobiles on each trip and 600+ passengers. We opted for a "luxury" room with bunk beds, a toilet, and an included meal. The toilet room can also be used to take a shower. I don't know how you'd accomplish that because the bathrooms are smaller than an airplane restroom if you can imagine that. I hope they check the restrooms after each trip because there could be an "oversized" person wedged in one of them!

Did you know that there are hundreds of railroad crossings between Virginia and Florida... and the train blows its whistle at each and every one of them? I tried to sleep after drinking a lot of wine, but I don't think I got more than a few moments of sleep during the entire 17-hour overnight trip. I'm still recovering from the ordeal!

We haven't taken another train ride since that Auto Train trip. Based on that experience, we may never take another again. But, as they say... never say never!

THE VILLAGES

Our retirement community is unique. It has been billed as both 'America's friendliest hometown' and 'America's healthiest hometown.' If you listen to the video that is provided by The Villages, the musical jingle gets stuck in your head once you hear it, and you remember it forever. Pure genius on the part of the advertising department.

One of my favorite stories was when we came to The Villages and bought our first place. It was the day after closing on our new 'Jasmine' designer home. We had purchased a minimum amount of furniture to get us started, which was delivered on the day of closing. We spent the first night in our new house with a bedroom set, a couch, and a couple of great room chairs. The following morning, I got dressed and headed out to Starbucks for a couple of coffees and some danish pastries. We didn't even have a coffee maker at this point. At Starbucks, I got in line and eventually ordered our drinks and eats. I prepared Brenda's coffee, as she liked it, with a little cream and some artificial sweetener. I like my coffee light, so I poured out a good portion of the black coffee to make room for my favorite vanilla-flavored creamer. A lady sitting nearby at a high-top table was observing my preparation of coffee and commented, "I see you like coffee with your cream!" I responded, "Yes, I do, but you'll notice I didn't put any sugar in it because I'm sweet enough already!" Her response… "I'll bet you are!" I think she was flirting with me. We exchanged smiles, and I left to head back to the house, thinking along the way that this truly was starting to feel like 'America's friendliest hometown!'

We eventually got our new southern home outfitted with more furniture. We bought a dining room table and six chairs from a used furniture place called Bargains and Treasures. Some years later, we resold that table and four chairs (we kept two as spares) on consignment through the same store for more than we originally purchased it! What a deal. I tell people that we went to every furniture store from Ocala to Orlando and every-where in between in our quest to outfit our 'southern palace.'

As we spent more and more time in The Villages, we met some really nice people. Hey, that's why they call it the 'friend-liest hometown.' We met an interesting guy by the name of Ralph, who did some interior painting for us. He, at one time, owned a painting company back in Long Island, New York, and did work for some of the most prestigious homes in 'The Hamptons.' That is a wealthy area at the east end of the island encompassing Southampton and East Hampton. Ralph had retired to The Villages but still did some painting. He also had formed a band of which he was the lead singer. His daughter was a prominent entertainer in church and theater and had a beautiful voice.

Ralph was doing a side gig one evening at a place on the corner of Sumter Landing, one of the three town squares in The Villages. The place was originally called Urban Flats before being changed to City Fire. This is a restaurant with a covered outdoor bar area where you can find people drinking beer and mixed drinks at 10 o'clock in the morning! It is definitely a hang-out and meeting place for, shall we say, socially active folks. It was not our place of choice, but Ralph invited us to come in and enjoy his one-man evening show. The Villages is host to people of all kinds of persuasions... singles, married couples, LGBQT, and everything in between. On this evening, we sat at the bar and ordered a glass of wine. As the entertainment began and people started to drift in, we noticed some ladies seated near us who were definitely on the prowl. The leather skirts and pants, makeup, and jewelry were obviously meant to attract. And attract they did. Men started circling like buzzards, checking out their prey. We were beginning to realize what this place was really all about... a pickup joint. It was like watching a bunch of college kids in heat. This was not the kind of fun we anticipated and we felt just a little out of place. It wasn't long before we finished our drinks, gave the nod to Ralph that we were leaving and headed home. I don't think we ever went back to City Fire, and our one-time venture there gave new meaning to 'America's friendliest hometown.' I guess there is something for everybody in this community. We obviously fit in better in other social circles. I always wondered, though, if any of the guys 'got lucky' that evening. Maybe it's best that I don't know.

A picture of our first house in The Villages, Florida. I made the mistake of sending some pictures to former co-workers at Pratt & Whitney. One of them had Photoshop capabilities and sent this picture back to us. Another view was with a nuclear facility behind the villa wall while we stood on our bare lot. We've had more than a few laughs every time we look at these pictures.

PROJECTS

I love to do projects. I have always been mechanically inclined, so even in my old age I still take on a project now and then. I pick and choose what I will work on next and hire out the rest. When I was rebuilding my airplane back in 1968, I had the training and confidence to do all the work myself. Later in life, I completed our house in Manchester, Connecticut. It was a six-month ordeal to obtain the certificate of occupancy. The partially completed house had sat through the winter with no heat. When I finally turned the water back on to check for leaks, I heard the water running but couldn't find any leaks ... until the water finally started coming out of the kitchen ceiling and cabinets! I discovered two split copper pipes upstairs that were the sources of the leaks. After repair, the water was again turned on with no additional leaks. Such are the joys of home ownership and doing your own repairs.

After completing the house and moving in, the next project was building a 1937 Ford hot rod. That took a full year of work to complete. I did all the bodywork, wiring, drive train installation, and driveway painting. Then came along a 1930 Ford roadster hot rod I bought from a guy in California. I rebuilt the exhaust system, installed a chopped soft top, and upholstered the rumble seat. Next was the building of my 1932 Ford hot rod. That turned out to be an eight-year project. Building this car happened about the time we were selling our Strawberry Lane house and having a new house built on Bella Vista Lane in Manchester. I would go to bed at night thinking about what I might do the next day on the project car. Then I'd get up and try to accomplish what I dreamed about the night before. We were always planner-type people and tried to leave nothing to chance. I think that is why we have accomplished so much in life without having too many hiccups.

Fast forward to retirement in The Villages, Florida. We are now on our second southern home. We have been told that most people who retire here buy, on average, three houses. The people that we bought our current house from had four (houses). They started with a small villa, then bought a designer home, then purchased the premier home we now live in, and then went back to a new designer home. They hadn't been in the latest designer home for more than a year when they sold it and moved back to Iowa. I think it had something to do with health issues. As we settled into our premier home, I still had two hot rods... a 1932 Ford coupe and a 1930 Ford roadster. About this time, I had owned the roadster for 20 years. It needed a refresh of everything from chrome to rubber hoses which seemed to deteriorate rapidly in the Florida heat and humidity. I finally decided to sell this car and enlisted the aid of Gateway Classic Cars in Orlando. We had a specialist detail the car before putting it on the market. He did a fantastic job buffing out the paint and it looked like a jewel when he was done. Someone up in Ohio must have thought it looked pretty good, too, because the car sold in a couple of weeks for over $42,000. After the sale of this hot rod, we purchased a BMW 230i convertible for Brenda. It was about time that she had her own car again. She proudly displays her car with the specialty license plate "No. 1 MAMA."

It was time for another project. I was never completely satisfied with the front brake system on the '32 Ford. It consisted of Buick 12" drums and old Lincoln backing plates. I had made numerous attempts to correct some issues with this brake system but was never completely satisfied with the results. After complaining for years about this, Brenda finally told me to just fix it so she wouldn't have to listen to me bitching about it. I purchased a $2,200 front brake kit from SoCal Speed shop in California. It looked exactly like the old-school system but incorporated hidden four-piston calipers underneath the polished aluminum drums. It took me a month or so to retrofit this new brake system onto the car but I savored each step of the process. I remember sweating a lot in the heat and humidity of a Florida summer. Sometimes, the hardest part of the project was getting up off the garage floor! Trust me, at an advanced age, this task is not as easy as it looks. The bottom line is that I completed the project, and the new brake system looks and works fantastic. Driving the car is now a pleasure again. "Stops on a dime and gives you two cents change!"

Our new 2022 Yamaha gas golf cart is really nice and a pleasure to drive. It is almost as quiet as an electric cart. One thing really pissed me off about it, though, and that was the front wheels. Having built a couple of cars from scratch, I knew a thing or two about front-end alignment. Castor, camber, and tow-in are important adjustments on any vehicle. These new Yamaha carts had a chassis redesign starting with the 2017 model year. As a result, the front wheels came from the factory with negative camber, so much so that they looked like a race car purposely set up for a short track with lots of left turns. I could spot these new carts a mile away just from the negative camber. We approached two of the dealerships in The Villages, and they could do nothing about the camber problem. That's the way they came from the factory and there were no adjustments for this problem. They said it was for stability on the golf course, but we drive these carts thousands of miles a year on pavement. Tire wear would certainly be an issue. My research for an aftermarket fix led me to a company selling adjustable coil-over shocks that would fix the camber problem. I ordered the new shocks for $175 and began the process of installing them soon after they arrived. Again, the hardest part of doing a project like this was getting up off the garage floor! Damn, it just keeps getting harder and harder, but I was determined to fix the camber problem. After some trial and error, I got the new shocks installed. The front wheels now had a little positive camber and just a little tow-in. The cart drives perfectly with this new setup, our tires will last longer, and I had the satisfaction of doing the job myself. Another project completed. What will be the next project?

I had spotted a picture of a garage online that was painted in a two-tone dark and light gray. I got the itch to take on this project next since our garage was painted in the builder-supplied flat white. After deciding on the color scheme with my wife, Brenda, the paint was purchased, and the work began. This turned out to be a three-week project. I had a lot of memorabilia on the walls, so much so that I took pictures of them before disassembling and painting so I could get them all back in the same locations. Lots of masking tape was used around obstacles like the two circuit breaker panels and the whole house vacuum system. I completed the job just in time for the neighborhood driveway party to be held at our house. I think people were impressed with the garage because they asked if they needed to take their shoes off before entering. I must have done a good job on this project and am already looking for another one. I'm sure one will pop into my head before too long! I guess I love to do projects!

DUI

I had been taught from a very young age to respect police men and women. We are a nation of laws and we would be a third world country without them. Ironically, our son Brett became a police officer in Stamford, Connecticut and is in his 26th year of service as of this writing. Disrespect for cops has been a trend in recent years for a number of reasons starting with the top law enforcement agent in the country, the attorney general. The system has become corrupt and politically weaponized. It is a two tiered justice system with a different set of rules for the elite who are politically connected. Hopefully, this will be corrected after the 2024 election.

Having said that, my first brush with the law was in California, where I was going to college back in 1966 and 1967. I had a Honda scrambler motorcycle which was my main mode of transportation. I removed the exhaust pipe mufflers to get a little more performance out of the bike. Driving along

Hawthorne Boulevard one day I spotted a motorcycle cop in my rear view mirror. He was looking right up my tail pipes. His lights came on and he pulled me over. I got a ticket for the loud, open exhaust system. The next day I put the mufflers back in the exhaust pipes and got it inspected. I had to appear in court with the paperwork showing compliance. The judge showed a little compassion and kicked me out of his courtroom without a fine. I got lucky, but still had respect for the law.

It would be years later before I had another encounter with the police. I had been working 2nd shift engineering at the Middletown, Connecticut Pratt & Whitney facility and was on my way home at around 1:30 AM. As I drove through Glastonbury, a vehicle rapidly approached me from behind and came almost up to my rear bumper. This really got my attention because I thought I was dealing with a drunk driver. Before too long, blue lights were flashing and I realized that this was a cop. What the hell was he stopping me for? I pulled over, rolled down my window and presented my license and registration. "What did you stop me for, officer? I'm on my way home from work." The officer replied "you were weaving from side to side." Hell, you'd weave from side to side if you were watching what you thought was a drunk driver on your rear bumper, too. I told him "must be a slow night in Glastonbury, officer!" I guess he didn't appreciate that comment because he wrote me a ticket for 'failure to drive right.' You gotta be kidding me! The incident pissed me off so much that I wrote a scathing letter to the mayor and chief of police reporting this officer for his heavy handed tactics, which I thought were uncalled for. Glastonbury Boulevard was a known area for traffic stops. I had been stopped a couple of times before and let go with no ticket. They were looking for drunks coming home from bars. Not much else happens in the bedroom community of Glastonbury, so this is how the police generate income to justify their existence.

Not a DUI occasion, but I often think of when we sold our house in Connecticut and were transitioning to our retirement house in Florida. We sold most things we were not taking with us at a garage sale. Anything that we did not sell, we either gave to our kids or donated to charity. Many of our prized possessions were loaded into our SUV for the trip south including important paperwork, computer, jewelry, guns, ammunition, booze, and our moonshine from West Virginia. I drove the first leg of the trip which got us down into Virginia. Brenda took over the driving duties as evening set in. I was tired and reclined my seat to catch a little sleep. As evening turned into night, Brenda chugged along. At some point I opened my eyes and looked over at Brenda to see how she was doing. She was cruising along just fine. We were approaching the state of North Carolina. About this time, I glanced at the instrument panel. She was cranking along at 80 to 85 mph! Ummmm, "I think you should dial it back a little bit, Brenda. If we get stopped for speeding and they find all the stuff we've got on board, we're going to jail for sure!" She backed down to a more reasonable speed and continued on. Those Virginia and Carolina state police were notorious for pulling over out of state vehicles. We may have dodged a bullet.

After our retirement to Florida, we were visiting our kids and grand kids in Connecticut one summer. We had been at our daughter's house in Tolland and were on our way back to the hotel in Manchester. I had had a few glasses of wine, or was it six? I don't remember exactly but I was feeling no pain, but felt I was good enough to drive. I may even drive better after a few drinks, maybe not. Anyhow, as we approached our exit on the highway, we noticed lots of lights on the overpass. I concluded that it must be night time construction taking place. We took the off ramp and circled around to go over the bridge. Oh, no! It was a DUI check point, and now I couldn't turn around to avoid it. I was stopped by an officer and rolled down my window. "Where are you coming from? Have you had anything to drink?" Being honest, I responded that we had been at our daughter's house and I had, maybe, one glass of wine. I have learned since then that you NEVER say you've had anything to drink. Of course, I was then put through the obligatory eye test with a flashlight checking for "Nystagmus" or involuntary movement of the eyes. I must have done pretty good on the test because the officer said "OK, you're free to go." Holy shit, what a relief! I passed a DUI roadside test after having six glasses of wine! I called my son, the cop, and told him of my accomplishment. He didn't see the humor in it.

My next interaction with the police was while driving our golf cart in our retirement community in Florida. I had passed another cart and violated the 20 mph rule. I was doing 27 mph and got caught on radar. The ticket was not for speeding, it was for driving an unregistered vehicle. The infraction was a criminal misdemeanor, must appear in court. I didn't give the officer any crap because I just had a beer after golf. At least I learned what not to say in an incident like this. After a $450 fine for court costs and probation officer fees, I learned my lesson. Maybe. I now have a rap sheet about one inch long. I'm a bad boy. I've heard that some women like bad boys. Just saying. Anyhow, I think the incident makes for an interesting story. It's always good for a few laughs. Hopefully, I'm done with all of my brushes with the law. Maybe not. Calls for defunding the police are ridiculous. The police are necessary to uphold the law and protect us from the bad guys. I still have the utmost respect for them.

BUSHNELL

As I mentioned in another short story, I had been stopped by a Sumter County sheriff for traveling more than 20 mph in our golf cart. It was after a round of golf. We had had a beer. Dexter and I were headed home on the golf cart path at the edge of the boulevard. I had just overtaken another golf cart when an officer captured us on his radar gun from a side street. We were not cited for traveling over the speed limit at 27 mph, but rather for driving an unregistered vehicle outside the golf cart lane. The infraction was considered a criminal misdemeanor requiring a visit before the judge in Bushnell. The officer did give me a break and recommended that I have The Villages golf cart repair shop adjust the governor back down to 20 mph. It would work in my favor if I presented the paperwork to the judge.

Modifying the governor was easy. All one had to do was take a plastic tie wrap, place it around the spring-loaded governor, and cinch it up to increase the engine's speed. This could increase the cart's speed from 20 mph to 30 mph. To undo it, simply cut the tie wrap. Because the repair shop needed to verify the speed, it cost $30 to transport the cart back and forth to the shop and another $70 for labor.

The court date was fast approaching, so Brenda and I drove down to Bushnell for a dry run to find the location of the courthouse. I didn't want to be late for my appearance. Traveling on county road 301 took us past old farms, swamps, abandoned houses and trailers, and generally 'old Florida' countryside. After a half-hour of driving, we came around a bend in the road, and in front of us was this opulent building. That must be the courthouse! It became immediately apparent that this is where all the money from traffic stops in The Villages was going. Somebody has to pay for the sheriffs, judges, and lawyers, and this time, I guessed, it was going to be me.

On the appointed day, I arrived at the courthouse and was directed to the courtroom where my case was going to be heard. I was not alone. There had to be at least 50 other people in the courtroom. As the cases were being called before the judge, a little old man with a walker and his wife approached the judge. It turns out he had been cited for the same infraction as me. In fact, there were at least eight cases involving speeding in a golf cart on this day. Excuse me, driving an unregistered vehicle. Finally, it was my turn. I presented the paperwork from the repair shop. The judge mentioned that he processes over 200 of these cases a year. How do you plead? No contest. As the gavel struck, I was directed to go to the cashier and pay court costs amounting to $300. Then, I was directed to go down the street to the probation office building to arrange costs associated with six months of probation. You gotta be kidding me!

I was pretty pissed off at this point, but I walked to the probation building and handed in my court paperwork. When my name was called, I was told I would have to come back after my six months of probation and the cost would be $50 at that time. I was pretty adamant that there was no way I was coming back. Just let me pay the fine now and let me out of here. They conceded but would not accept a check. I came prepared and whipped out $50 cash. They wouldn't accept cash either. "What the hell will you accept?" A money order. Okay, I'll play the game. "Where do I get a money order?" You can get them at the gas station/convenience store down the street. "Okay, I'll be right back." As I walked to the convenience store, guess who I passed? It was the little old guy with his walker and his wife! Geez, they were making him go through this charade also!

The money order was secured for a $5 service fee (of course) and I headed back to the probation office. The little old man was still making his way to the convenience store. Poor guy. After paying my $50 with the money order, I was finally out of there and on my way home. Between golf cart service, court, and probation costs, this turned out to be a $450 ordeal. Bottom line? Don't speed in your golf cart. Well, I actually still do but I do it with a multitude of caution. I surely don't want to be a repeat offender. The judge might throw the book at me. It might cost even more the next time! Now I have a rap sheet a half inch long! I've heard that some girls like bad boys like me. Maybe not.

GOLF

I have never had a hole-in-one, and I've been golfing off and on since I was 15 years old. That's over 60 years of trying. I've come close more than a few times, mind you, but the ball always refused to fall in the hole. I've had three eagles, which, to me, are like a hole-in-one. I only saw one of them actually drop in the hole. The others were over a ridge and out of sight. Most people that I golf with have had at least one hole-in-one. Many of the women in our various social circles have had multiple one-timers. I'm thinking I may go through this life without ever scoring the elusive ONE.

When you golf for as long as I have, there will inevitably be stories to tell. Some of the stories I'd like to forget like the time I was working 3rd shift and decided to play nine holes after I had been up all night. I went to our local Twin Hills CC in Coventry, Connecticut, and jumped into an open tee time slot with a couple of other folks. My mom and pop partners were old. Probably in their early 80s, I guessed. They each carried cloth bags with maybe four or five clubs and walked the course. I had a wheeled cart to haul my full set of clubs with me. I let the old couple tee off first. Age before beauty. They didn't hit the ball too far, maybe 100 yards, but right down the middle of the fairway. My tee shot went a booming 225 yards, slicing off into the adjacent cow pasture. This round was not starting off as I had planned. After a drop and a chunked second shot, I was beginning to think golfing after being up all night was probably not a great idea. Long story short, the old folks kicked my ass all away around the course. I was beginning to hate old people who had game. Maybe I should have just hung it up for the day. I never tried to play golf again after working a 3rd shift.

Our son, Brett, and one of his buddies challenged me and Brenda's cousin, Bob Desjardins, to a match. We met at Goodwin Park in Hartford. They were young, hit the ball a ton, and felt optimistic that they could beat the old guys. We scored pretty evenly at the start of the game, but the old guys started pulling ahead as the round progressed. The boys were getting a little frustrated, so they started swinging harder. On the next tee, Brett's friend was up next. He teed the ball up high, positioned it forward in his stance, and took a mighty swing with his driver. It sounded like the club head broke the sound barrier. The ball popped straight up into the air and must have had a tremendous amount of backspin because when it hit the ground, it took off and ended up 20 yards behind us! Damn! That's the first time I've ever seen that happen! Long story short ... the old guys ruled that day.

On another occasion, Bob and I played the East Hartford golf course. We were on the back nine and had just teed off. We hopped into the golf cart, and as we approached our balls, we spotted a driver's head cover on the ground next to the cart path. It looked like a wild animal lying there. So what did Bob do? He jammed on the brakes, jumped out, pounced on the 'animal,' and started wrestling with it on the ground! The group in front of us looked back and couldn't believe what they were seeing. I was laughing my ass off. When we caught up to the group in front of us, Bob gave them back the club head cover and said, "He put up a mean fight and almost got the best of me!" The other players just looked at each other, shook their heads, and moved on.

I've never been a long hitter. My best drive ever was about 235 yards, but it was downhill, downwind, and landed on a hard pan surface. I'm guessing the mechanics of my swing had something to do with it. I just couldn't deliver enough club head speed to hit long distances. Don't get me wrong, I've played some pretty good golf in my prime. My handicap was about 12 for a time and I shot some rounds in the high 70s. I've taken lessons from PGA teaching pros and learned some good techniques. I had my swing speed checked recently before buying a new set of clubs so I could select the right shaft for me. I figured my speed would be clocked at around 80 or 85 mph. The swing speed meter recorded 60 mph! Could I have slowed down that much in my old age? The answer is "yes."

Over the years, I have regressed from teeing off on the black tips to the blues to the whites and more recently, the green tees. I suppose someday I'll be moving up to the friendly tees if I'm still alive. Golf has become less competitive for me in my old age. I hardly ever play championship courses anymore, playing executive courses only once or twice a week. My wife, Brenda, golfs with me from time to time, and we play with other couples on occasion. Usually, the game is 'best ball,' which makes for a really relaxing round of golf. No pressure. Just hit the ball as best you can and enjoy the scenery and conversation. We have a lot of golf courses to choose from in our retirement community of The Villages. Fifty-six and counting as we speak.

There are many other stories that could be told, but like they say about Vegas, 'what happens on the golf course stays on the golf course!' I have lots of memories from playing this game and I'm hoping there will be lots more in my future. My dad never played golf. He told me he was going to take up the game when he got old. He never did. Probably a good thing. He avoided all the frustration associated with the game. Smart man.

Did I mention that I've never had a hole-in-one? I thought so.

Golf Carts

Living in a retirement community like The Villages in central Florida is interesting. There are a lot of old people here in 'God's waiting room' as one friend so eloquently stated. They are from all walks of life, as you might expect, and all levels of acuity. In a community that is approaching 150,000 in population, you'd expect that there would be some anomalies from time to time, and driving incidents are near the top of the list. Old people can be on all kinds of medications for all kinds of health issues. Many should be medicated but are not, or maybe they have forgotten to take their meds. In any case, these people drive golf carts, bikes, motorcycles, and cars. It is inevitable that some of them will have an accident sooner or later. Usually sooner.

Golf carts are the primary mode of transportation. There are electric carts, gas carts, hot rod carts and custom carts of every description. The cost of these can range from a few thousand dollars to $25,000 or more for a custom cart. Some people put thousands of miles on them every year. You can do your shopping in one, go to doctor appointments, golf, drive around the town squares at night, go to activities such as pickleball, or just cruise The Villages. The list is endless. The speed limit for them is 20 mph, but the governor can be overridden, resulting in a breathtaking 30 mph! I have personal experience with this since I modified our golf cart engine years ago. It's pretty easy to do, and I was getting tired of little old ladies passing me in their hopped-up carts. A buddy and I had just finished a round of golf, had a beer, and were on our way home. We were traveling on the cart path at the edge of a boulevard when we approached a slower-moving golf cart with two cue tips (old people with white or silver hair) in it. With no automobile traffic behind me, I proceeded to accelerate and pass these old coots. Just as I cleared them and started to pull back into the cart path lane, I spotted a sheriff's car on the edge of the road. He spotted me also... with a radar gun pointed in my direction! His lights came on, and we were pulled over. I seem to remember that the cue tips gave us the middle finger as they slowly passed us. How embarrassing! Anyhow, the cop cited me for traveling at the unbelievable speed of 27 mph. The ticket wasn't for speeding, though; it was for driving an unlicensed vehicle, which is a criminal misdemeanor, requiring an appearance in court. Long story short, court expenses were $450 with six months of probation. Lesson learned. Well, maybe not. I'm just a little more aware of where the speed traps are now and more careful of my speed. Can't have those old ladies passing me!

In The Villages, we are told that many people get hurt in golf cart accidents. Each year, as many as five people are reportedly killed. Some of the accidents are caused by speed and loss of control and some are because of collisions with cars. One prime example is our realtor lady who helped us buy our first house here. She was golfing with a friend when he took an abrupt turn, and she fell out of the cart, hitting her head in the process. She was out of work for an extended period because of the accident and tried to make a comeback as a Village salesperson. The head injury finally resulted in her losing her life. What a beautiful lady. What a terrible loss.

On a lighter note, we have a pickleball friend by the name of Kubota Bill. He got that name because he was a farm boy from the upper Midwest and his golf cart was painted in camouflage. After a party one evening and a few too many drinks, Bill was on his way home in his camo cart. Somehow, he got off the cart path and onto one of the main roads. He was spotted by a local sheriff's deputy who went after him with lights and sirens. As they approached a roundabout, of which we have many in The Villages, Bill sped up, going around and around, trying to outrun the cop! When Bill finally gave up and pulled over, he told the officer that he was just trying to get out of his way. The officer laughed, took pity on him, and directed him back to the cart path. Not only did the sheriff get Bill back on a cart path along the edge of the road, he followed him all the way back to his house! No ticket? Bill got lucky that evening.

DANCING

I was never much of a dancer. One of my early attempts was when I was about 13 or 14. A school dance was on the horizon, and a parent of one of the girls in my class thought it would be a good idea to give a dance lesson. And so, we met at the girl's house and went to the basement for the lesson. I still remember to this day one of the songs that was played. It was Mr. Sandman by the Chordettes. "Mr. Sandman, bring me a dream. Make him the cutest that I've ever seen." I couldn't get my feet to move to this music for some reason and years later, every time I hear that song, I still can't get my feet to move to that music! I think that song ruined my dancing career for life.

Over the years, Brenda and I danced at special occasions like wedding receptions and the like, but nothing more serious than a slow dance or an attempt at a rock & roll favorite. Brenda always expressed a desire to dance. But me, not so much. I eventually got talked into taking country partner dance lessons after work at the Pratt & Whitney Aircraft Club on Clement Road in East Hartford, Connecticut. Our instructors were Bill and Miriam Cover. He was an excellent teacher, and we learned a lot from this couple. We met Bob and Charlotte White at this venue and became lifelong friends. They are the couple that introduced us to The Villages retirement community. We got pretty good at country dancing and performed with the group at county fairs, senior centers, and weekend group gatherings. We all had the same outfits, hats, and boots. We also learned line dancing and two-step. We had memorized 60 or more different dance routines. At one time, we were dancing four nights a week while also holding down full-time jobs.

There was one couple that we always got a chuckle out of. They had all the hand and arm movements but just couldn't get their feet to move to the beat of the music. To this day, every time we see someone on the dance floor and their feet are not synchronized to the beat of the music, it brings back memories of that couple. After our retirement to The Villages, Florida, we saw a couple dancing in the town square. They were swing dancing. They were smooth and made it look so easy. It was fun to watch and, I suppose, probably fun to do. I wanted to learn how to do the East Coast swing, so I made a deal with Brenda. If she would take up golf, I would take up swing dancing. She agreed, and we started to take weekly lessons at one of the recreation centers with Kermit and Carol. We learned some really nice moves from this couple, and we still do most of them to this day. We are not ballroom dancers, which is nice, but too formal for us. We like informal and fun dances, including country partner, line, swing, two-step, cha cha, and waltz. And, yes, we do a little buckle rubbing, also known as slow dancing.

One of my favorite memories is going on a country cruise to the Caribbean. I was dancing with Charlotte. I raised up my arm to lead her into a turn. She kept turning and turning and turning. I needed to learn to be a stronger lead and bring my arm down to signal her to stop turning! Another lesson that we still laugh about to this day.

Talking about dancing would not be complete without a story my dad told me years ago. As the story goes, he was at a school dance. A guy that my dad knew, who we will call Fred, had a bad speech impediment. He kind of slurred his words. This story sounds better if you tell it verbally using the slur, but you can just use your imagination for this reenactment. In the old days, all the guys lined up on one side of the dance floor and all the girls on the other. Fred had his eye on one girl in particular, so when he got brave enough, he went over to her to ask her to dance. She turned him down. After a number of attempts to ask her to dance and getting rebuffed, he finally told her to "kiss my ass!" The girl got upset and told her older brother who was also at the dance. They approached Fred and confronted him. Fred responded, "Did I tell you to kiss my ass?" The girl said, "Yes, you certainly did!" Fred replied after considering his options, "Well, you don't hafta!" The story ends there, and I don't know if Fred avoided getting punched out by the older brother. True story. Probably funnier in person.

Brenda and I still dance to this day whenever we can. We dance at the Amigo's Sports Club monthly dances and the town squares when our favorite John Dixon Band plays. This country group used to be called the Lee Ann Noel Band. Lee Ann was the band's drummer and one of the singers. She learned her trade in the honky-tonk bars of Texas and brought this knowledge to The Villages. She knew what country folk liked to dance to and played a variety of music to please her audience. Tragically, Lee Ann died after a fight with throat cancer. Her lead singer and guitarist, John Dixon, took over the band and continues in her tradition.

WEATHER

Having been born and brought up in Massachusetts, we never thought too much about weather. Summers could be as hot and humid as Florida at times. Sometimes it was even MORE hot and humid than Florida! Fall was a nice time of year with cooler, dryer weather, trees turning a myriad of colors, and the time-honored practice of raking leaves. When I was a kid in the 1940s and 1950s, we were still allowed to rake the leaves to the curb and burn them. The smell of burning leaves could last for weeks as people cleaned up their yards. It wasn't long before the environmentalists got involved and laws were passed prohibiting this practice. The fallback (pun intended) method was to rake the leaves into a pile, drag them with a tarp to the edge of your property, and dump them. The rotting leaves always resulted in rich soil where we could dig up night crawlers for fishing.

Fall was nice but short-lived. You always knew what was coming next... winter. I seem to remember that winters were harsher back then. We had to shovel all that white stuff by hand. We never owned a snow blower. It was a monumental task getting the big driveway cleared. Mounds of snow at the edge of the driveway would last well into spring. I still remember the delivery of milk from our local farmer. They were delivered once or twice a week in glass bottles and placed in an insulated metal box near the back door. In cold weather, the frozen milk would pop the cap forming a stalagmite up to two inches tall. Milk is still delivered in glass bottles in some areas of the country. Environmentalists must like this method because it cuts down on the use of plastic and paper cartons. What's old has become new again.

Somehow we survived until spring had sprung. After a cold winter, a sunny, fifty-degree day was cause for celebration. We'd be outside in tee shirts working in the yard with mounds of snow remaining everywhere. Brenda and I got married on April 18, 1969. We traveled to New Hampshire and Vermont on our honeymoon for spring skiing. It felt so warm, we didn't even need a jacket. What a nice time of year... sometimes. Springtime in New England still brought some bad weather once in a while... more often than we liked. It was not uncommon to experience a full week of rain and clouds without ever seeing the sun. Bummer. It's a good thing we had to go to work. At least then we could ignore the lousy weather and pass the time of day earning a living.

Fast forward to retirement in Florida. Admittedly, we do get some cold weather here in January and February. Hell, we even had a couple of nights down to 26 degrees recently. That is cold by Florida standards. But not long after a cold snap, we would be right back up to 70 degrees and sunny. There is a reason they call this the Sunshine State. Even though central Florida is considered tropical, we have, on occasion, up to four temperature zones ranging from the 80s in the Keys to the 50s up in Pensacola. Our local newspaper, the Daily Sun, always has a colorful temperature map of the country. Sometimes, when Florida is painted yellow and orange, the rest of the nation is painted blue. I take this opportunity to snap a picture of the map and post it on Facebook, stating, "The reason we live in Florida!" Some people hate me for doing this. Some admire our decision to live here. We keep our saltwater pool at 90 degrees all winter long. I swim 100 laps every day. We don't call it skinny dipping. We call it chunky dunking because of our mature bodies. This might be too much information (TMI) for some readers to comprehend. Bottom line... if we had to go back to New England in the wintertime after our blood has thinned out here in Florida... we'd die.

Summers can be hot in Florida. That's why there are snowbirds. Snowbirds come down from the northern regions for six months and then migrate back up north for summer. They can't stand the summer heat here. Snowflakes come down for just a couple of the colder northern months. In New England, a heat wave is considered three consecutive days of 90 degrees or more. In Florida, the whole summer is a heat wave. We are considered frogs because we live in the tropics full-time. We are going to croak here. You've gotta be tough to live down south all year round. 'Nuff said.

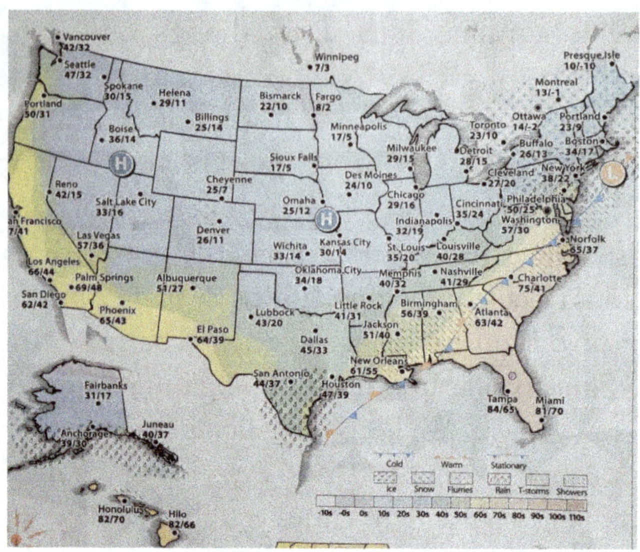

Our Daily Sun newspaper publishes a colorized weather map in every issue. During the colder months of the year, Florida stands out as the warmest spot in the nation and is colored orange while the rest of the nation is blue, indicating really cold weather. For some reason, I cannot resist the urge to take a picture of the map and display it on Facebook! I get varying degrees of responses from friends that either envy us or want to kill us!

SKY

When I was growing up in central Massachusetts, my eyes were always drawn to the sky. We had a small airport near us and I was intrigued watching the airplanes fly overhead. One neighbor buzzed his parents' house down the street from time to time. I got a real thrill out of that. From an early age, when an airplane flew over, I would watch it until it was out of sight. I even drove my bicycle into the brush at the side of the road once because I couldn't take my eyes off an airplane. I was too young and foolish to just stop and watch it! My early love of airplanes led me to a career in aviation.

My dad always loved to be out on the porch during thunderstorms. He'd watch the lightning and count the seconds until the thunder reached us to determine the distance. The speed of sound is approximately 1,100 feet per second, so every 5 seconds was equal to one mile. In this way, you could determine how far away the lightning strike was when you heard the thunder that followed. It was a fun thing to do. When golfing, if lightning is within seven miles, the recommendation is to take cover because it is so unpredictable. Lee Trevino, the pro golfer, was hit by lightning once during a tournament. When a storm approached during another PGA event, he was warned by officials to take cover. What did Lee do? He pulled a one-iron out of his bag, held it up, and declared, "Even God can't hit a one-iron!" That was classic Lee Trevino.

When I was a young lad, my dad pointed out a comet to me in the night sky. He said it was Haley's comet, but my recent research reveals that it could not have been. It must have been another comet that was, indeed, visible to the naked eye. It was very interesting to a young kid who was curious and always looking to the sky. Street and house lights were minimal back in the day which made it easy to view the stars. This has become a problem over time as the population and cities have grown to produce more nighttime light pollution. I'm guessing it's probably still not a problem in rural "big sky" Montana.

I remember, as a kid, just lying on the lawn with a friend and looking at the daytime clouds. We used our imagination to see shapes that resembled animals or cartoon characters. An innocent way to pass the time.

Now retired in Florida, one of my favorite things to do is to relax in the hot tub at 5:00 in the morning and look at the planets, stars, and moving satellites overhead. Meteor showers are a real treat, and the more active ones produce 20 or 30 an hour. The Perseid showers peak in mid-August and the Geminids peak in mid-December. Meteoroids enter our atmosphere at an astonishing 27,000 to 90,000 mph. No wonder they burn up upon entry! I have an app on my phone called Skyview. When this app is turned on and pointed to the sky, it identifies all the planets. Venus is the brightest and most easily identified. The app also tracks the International Space Station (ISS). We witnessed it flying over the Tampa Bay Superbowl in the year 2021. Early one morning I was treated to a large, slow, double meteor burning up in the sky. Come to find out it might not have been a meteor after all. The ISS jettisons its toilet waste from time to time, and it gets burnt up reentering the atmosphere. Just a fun fact of life. Even if that large, slow, double streak of light was crap burning up in the atmosphere, it was still spectacular to watch!

I was recently treated to a real show one morning from the hot tub. I spotted a satellite moving overhead, followed by another, and then another. I counted 23 total. From my research, it turns out that Space X had just launched a rocket with Starlink satellites on board. They were released into low orbit and continued on a trajectory to approximately 380 miles of altitude. Once there, they unfold their solar panels and can be maneuvered using krypton-powered thrusters. This is like something out of a science fiction movie script. Fascinating technology. The satellites have a five-year life span and then fall out of orbit. With thousands of these floating around, they should provide some spectacular light shows as they burn up in the atmosphere in the future.

Speaking of the ISS, it recently jettisoned a big pallet of batteries that were supposed to burn up upon reentry. Most of them did, but a chunk made it all the way to Earth and punched a hole in the roof of a house in Naples, Florida! Fortunately, no one was injured. Almost 10,000 satellites have been launched into orbit for communication, weather, military, and spy reasons. Some of those satellites give us Global Positioning System (GPS) coordinates to locate where we are, map trip directions and plot the speed of our vehicles. Great technology that we use every day and could probably now not live without. Some satellites are traveling at the same pace as the earth's rotation, so they appear stationary. These are called Geosynchronous or Geostationary satellites. Some satellites are moving. The ISS, as an example, circles the globe approximately 16 times a day. It can be seen frequently in the night sky.

Many of the satellites are launched from the Kennedy Space Center in Florida. Sometimes they launch astronauts and supplies to the ISS. It is 85 miles as the crow flies from where we live in The Villages to Cape Canaveral. On a clear day or night, you can see a rocket being launched that far away. Years ago, booster rockets splashed down in the ocean and were not retrievable. With today's technology, the boosters land themselves, either back at the space center or on a large platform out at sea. Sometimes, a sonic boom can be heard, something we have not heard for quite a while. By my calculations, the "boom" takes about six or seven minutes to get to us, but it is still perceptible. Military jets used to break the sound barrier over land all the time when we were kids. The Federal Aviation Administration (FAA) finally prohibited them from doing so over land in 1973. The Concorde supersonic passenger plane was only allowed to break the sound barrier over the ocean but not over land. The plane was conceived in the 1960s and flew its final flight in 2003.

We were recently treated to a partial eclipse of the sun. Folks in the south-central United States got a view of the full eclipse, as did others in a path that extended up to New England. I have seen a number of eclipses in my lifetime and always appreciated the uniqueness of an event like this. And, yes, we used special glasses that a friend provided to view the eclipse. We didn't want to burn out our retinas!

I will continue to look skyward and try to identify airplanes that fly overhead. It's something I have done my entire life. One time recently a WWII B-17 bomber flew over The Villages. It was flying a tour of the country and stopped at our local Leesburg Airport. Tragically, that airplane crashed and killed the pilot, copilot, and some of the paying passengers while flying a demonstration flight out of Bradley Airport in Connecticut. On another occasion, a L39 Czech military trainer jet made some low passes over our neighborhood. It must have come from Leesburg or the flight training center down at Kissimmee Gateway Airport. On his last pass, he did a slow roll while climbing back up to altitude. Of course, I watched it until it was out of site. Old habits don't die easily.

WACO

Real airplanes have round engines and two wings. Some endearing soul made that statement many years ago. It refers to biplanes that have been in existence since the early days of aviation and were first flown by the Wright brothers in 1903. The 'round engine' words refer to radial engines, which became popular and mass-produced during the 1920s. They consisted of a crankcase with attached cylinders arranged in a radial pattern. The air-cooled cylinders were always of an odd number because of timing and balance design concerns, so it was common to see an engine with seven or nine cylinders. Biplanes were phased out after WWII in favor of faster and more efficient monoplanes. Two-winged variants were still used for training purposes during the Great War but became surplus after the war. Surplus airplanes, like Stearman and Waco, could be purchased cheaply and many were used in the years that followed the war in agricultural spraying applications.

I've always appreciated these old airplanes for their nostalgic look, sound, and history. They were slower than monoplanes because of all the parasitic drag associated with two wings, large frontal area, struts, and flying wires. Many of these airplanes that survived years of usage are in private hands now or used for exhibition flying and aerobatics. Waco Aircraft in Battle Creek, Michigan is still producing modern versions of these old airplanes. If you've got a lot of money, you can still buy a new one!

I have a bucket list. Everybody probably has one, especially when they get older and are in their 'golden years.' The list consists of things that you've always wanted to do, but either didn't have the time or didn't have the money to fulfill the dream. I always wanted to fly in a biplane which was near the top of my bucket list. Research found a company, Florida Air Tours, on Merritt Island, near Cocoa Beach that offered flights in a 1937 Waco UPF-7 biplane. I had booked a flight with them around the time of our return from a cruise out of Port Canaveral, but the flight was canceled due to weather. Another flight was arranged. My wife, Brenda, and I drove down to Cocoa Beach a day before the scheduled flight. We stayed overnight in a hotel and walked the beach during the evening. We had been in the area before visiting the Kennedy Space Center, but never got to the beach.

The next morning, we checked out of the hotel and headed to Merritt Island Airport. The front cockpit of the Waco was wide enough to accommodate two people, but I was going to fly alone this time for an aerobatic flight. The control stick was reinstalled in the front for my benefit. My pilot in command was retired Lt. Col. John Black who had accumulated a few thousand hours of flight time in Air Force F15 aircraft. I would be in good hands. After takeoff, we flew over part of the Kennedy Space Center, where we saw a Space X booster that had returned to Earth and was sitting on a barge in Port Canaveral. We gained a little altitude, and the controls were handed over to me as we headed out over Cocoa Beach. Flying parallel to the beach, we announced our presence to the beach people below by emitting a smoke trail with the injection of oil into the exhaust. John took over the controls, put the nose down to build up speed, and executed a barrel roll. The next maneuvers were a couple of wingovers proceeded by a loop. I was in my element! The controls were again handed back to me as we turned back toward Merritt Island. On the way back, I was allowed to do a series of wingovers. After each one, I got more and more aggressive with steeper climbs and descents. The airplane was surprisingly easy to maneuver, and I loved every minute of this flight. As we approached the airport, John took over the controls and made a perfect wheel landing.

I finally got a flight in a biplane and quickly checked that item off my bucket list. I even have the video of this flight on a thumb drive so that I can relive the memory. Maybe I'll even post it on Facebook for all to see. You just gotta love those round engines and two wings!

I love airplanes. I flew an hour of aerobatics in this 1937 Waco biplane out of Merritt Island, Florida. My pilot in command was Lt. Col. John Black who once logged 3600 hours of flying time in the USAF F15 Eagle. I was definitely in good hands flying with this veteran. As the old saying goes, "real airplanes have round engines and two wings."

HELICOPTER

I've always loved all things aviation. It started when I was just a kid watching biplanes fly over from the nearby airport. One neighbor who made a career in the Navy used to buzz his parents' house down the street. In doing so, he came pretty close to our house as well. My dad used to comment that he almost took the chimney off our house!

Over the years, I have taken flying lessons and obtained my private pilot license. I've flown Cessna 140, 150, 152 and 172. I owned and rebuilt my clipped-wing Piper Cub. I checked myself out in an Aeronca Champ and I've flown a Schweitzer sailplane. I did some aerobatics in a Waco UPF7 biplane and a P51 Mustang, and I flew the right seat of a DeHaviland Beaver on floats. The one thing I had not flown after all these years was a helicopter. Never mind flying, I hadn't even had a ride in one. Now, my mom, Flora, who lived all her life in Clinton, Massachusetts, was getting along in her years. She was approaching the age of 93 and still living in the home she and my father built back in the 1940s. She was taken to the local hospital with an abdominal problem. They could only do so much for her there, so she was transported by helicopter to another hospital in Worcester. Mother knew that I had never flown in a helicopter but always wanted to, so she took the opportunity to tease me about it and say that she was the first to get a ride in one. Thanks, Mom! I always thought that was cute of her to see humor in the situation, even though she was going through some serious medical issues at the time. She passed away a week later due to age and complications with surgery. I loved that girl. She will be forever in my heart.

It was inevitable that I would eventually get a ride in one of those rotary-winged aircraft. I did not want to just get a ride in one, I wanted to fly it. How hard could it be because I already had flown a few hundred hours in fixed-wing aircraft? Searching around for a place to fly, I came across a flight training center at Kissimmee Gateway Airport in Florida that gave lessons in a French Cabri G2 helicopter. Arrangements were made, and I went there with my wife, Brenda. The pre-flight of the aircraft took almost an hour. The checklist was long, and there were many moving parts on this machine. My instructor and I finally took off and headed to a remote area for low-level training. Flying in a straight line was no problem, but the skills required at low levels and in hover were a little more complicated. It didn't take too long to get the hang of it, but it would take many more hours of training to get comfortable enough to handle a flight on my own. We headed back to the airport because of a pending storm approaching the area. We touched down just before the wind and rain hit the area. I got my logbook signed for the one-hour flight, and we headed home. I never went back for another lesson but was truly grateful for finally getting my hands on the controls of a helicopter. I'm hoping my mom in heaven got to be there with me. Mom, you were the first of us to fly in a helicopter and I thought of you during my first flight!

We have a neighbor, Chip Harper, living across the street from us here in Florida, who, was a Navy helicopter pilot. He went on to fly commercially out of Teterboro, New Jersey, for a bunch of years. He flew all kinds of business folks and famous people in and around one of the world's busiest and most dangerous areas to fly, New York City. He accumulated nearly 15,000 hours of flight time and I admire him for this accomplishment. Having personally been at the controls of one of these complicated machines for just one hour, I really can appreciate the skill of this pilot. Thank you, Chip, for your service.

Brenda and I pictured in front of a French Cabri G2 at Kissimmee Gateway Airport in Florida. I never had a ride in a helicopter, so I took a one hour lesson in this aircraft. Flying a rotor winged aircraft is definitely more difficult than flying a fixed wing airplane. There are so many moving parts and the one hour pre-flight check proved that to be true.

P51

On the occasion of one recent birthday, my wife Brenda gave me a card wishing me all the best and many happy returns. On the card, she listed three options with little open boxes next to them. She knew I had talked about these wishes in the past and she wanted me to pick one. They were:

Pick one:
( ) New big-screen TV
( ) New golf cart
( ) Flight in a P51 Mustang

I had a hard time deciding which one to pick, so I picked all three!! Number three, the P51 Mustang flight, was high on my bucket list. Retired Lt. Col. John Black, with whom I had recently flown in a Waco biplane, highly recommended it. He was one of the instructor pilots who also flew at Stallion 51 at Kissimmee Gateway Airport in Florida.

When Brenda gave me the okay to make an appointment, I was still a little hesitant. The cost for a half-hour flight was around $3,000, and a one-hour flight was in excess of $5,000. This was expensive relative to the $300 I had spent for a helicopter lesson. And I thought the helicopter price was steep at the time. The P51 price was in the stratosphere. Of course, these aircraft cost millions of dollars, so their flight time was necessarily high. I opted for the half-hour flight.

I was given the go-ahead by a higher authority (Brenda), so I made the call. The appointment was scheduled for a month away, taking into account the demand for flight instruction in these aircraft. The chief flight instructor of the business is Lee Lauderback, a man who has logged over 22,000 hours of flight time, 11,000 of which are in a P51 Mustang. He is the highest-time P51 pilot in the world. His company owns two Mustangs plus other aircraft like an AT6 Texan and an L39 fighter jet trainer. His Mustangs are named Crazy Horse I and Crazy Horse II. These are WWII aircraft converted to two-place versions for training purposes.

On the day of my flight, the weather was questionable, but Brenda and I decided to head down to Kissimmee Gateway anyhow. Upon our arrival, we were told that the weather would be good enough to fly and we were taken into a conference room for a briefing with Steve Larmore, my instructor pilot. We went over all the maneuvers I would like to fly and signed the waiver in case I got killed doing them. Nice feeling. Next, I was introduced to the airplane for pre-flight inspection. I would be flying The Little Witch because both Crazy Horse aircraft were down for maintenance. I was a little apprehensive as I got strapped into the cockpit and instructed how to use the canopy release if we had to bail out. I secretly prayed I wouldn't have to use either the canopy release or the parachute. The Little Witch was pulled out of the hangar, and my pilot in command went through the pre-flight checklist. I was still questioning if this was a good thing to do... until the engine started. When you hear and feel a 1,500-horsepower Merlin engine start, it really pumps you up to get into the air. I couldn't wait any longer... I was ready!

Taxiing to the active runway and run-up of the engine was uneventful. We were finally given clearance from the tower to take off, so we taxied out to the active runway and pointed the nose down the center line. Applying full power, we accelerated down the runway and lifted off. With landing gear up, we headed to the practice area. At 9,000 feet of altitude, the pilot handed me the controls. Level flight and shallow turns came first. Then, a stall with the power back and the nose up. Piece of cake. Little Witch flies like a dream and is light on the controls. Asked if I'd like to do a barrel roll... of course! Nose down, 175 mph, pull back, nose up, and slow roll to the right. Nice feeling. Let's do another one to the left... awesome! Aileron rolls were easy. No rudder required. Just pull up a little and apply full stick to the left or right. Great instructions from Steve. Wanna do a loop? Of course! Stick forward to gain speed, then stick back all the way. Over the top we went, pulling 4Gs in the recovery. That was the first time I had felt that many G forces. Not bad.

My next request was for a Cuban eight, which was granted. Into a loop first, and just over the top, the stick is relaxed, and a half roll initiated. I needed a little help leveling the wings at the top, but other than that, I completed my first half of a Cuban eight. Great feeling. Time to head back to the airport. Playing with and around the clouds and executing another roll on the way back was fun. We got permission from the tower to fly a military approach, which is a pass at 1,000 feet halfway down the runway and then a 360-degree turn to line up down the center line. My instructor managed the power settings, flaps, and landing gear but let me fly the plane all the way to touch-down and roll out. A perfect wheel landing. What a thrill. I got to taxi Little Witch back to the hangar. Shutdown. After a debrief in the conference room and an entry in my logbook, we said our goodbyes. Thrill of a lifetime. Sure glad I checked that box on my birthday card. Got a video of the flight as a remembrance.

PS: I got the big screen TV and a new golf cart also! Lucky guy!

The Mustang is a hot rod! I was fortunate to get my hands on the controls of The Little Witch to do some aerobatics. It was an expensive treat to fly this bird at $3000 for a half hour. I was allowed to stall it, do a barrel roll, do aileron rolls, fly a loop (4 G's on pull out), and complete a half Cuban eight. I was apprehensive until the 1500 horsepower Merlin engine started and then I was good to go. Steve, my pilot in command, even allowed me to fly a military break and wheel landing. This was the thrill of a lifetime!

PICKLEBALL

We were first introduced to the game of pickleball when we visited The Villages, Florida in 2003. Friends of ours, Bob and Charlotte, had a winter home here and influenced us to come to visit for a week on the Lifestyle Preview Program. This program provided us with a free round of golf, some Village bucks, which we could spend anywhere in The Villages, and a beautiful villa right on the golf course. There was no pressure to purchase a home or villa here, but part of the program provided a nice trolley tour of the new retirement community which we took advantage of. One of the stops was at The Savannah Center, which consisted of a beautiful building with conference and meeting rooms, a computer room, and a 900-seat auditorium. Nearby was a recreation center with a pool, tennis courts, and pickleball courts.

Later in the week, we paid a visit to the recreation center. A couple took pity on us and introduced us to the new game of pickleball. The game was actually invented by a couple of folks in the state of Washington in 1965. They used a lowered badminton net, ping pong paddles, and wiffle balls made of plastic. Their dog, Pickles, apparently retrieved stray balls. And thus, the game was born. We weren't ready to buy a retirement home at this time in our lives and we didn't play the game of pickleball again for a number of years.

Fast forward to 2009. I had retired by this time and Brenda was closing in on retirement, so we took a Christmas break and returned to Florida for a vacation. We checked out Naples, Tampa/St. Pete, and Spring Hill on the West Coast but ended up back in The Villages for another visit with the Lifestyle Program. We made up our minds on this visit to purchase a new home here and put our 'money where our mouth was,' as the saying goes. Our realtor took a picture of us standing on our bare lot. I made the mistake of sending this picture to fellow former workers at Pratt & Whitney. We received the picture back after being photo shopped by a creative engineer. Now there was a nuclear power plant behind us in one photo and a 747 airplane landing behind us in another! These were my friends just trying to be funny. I think it's actually pretty hilarious.

Our house was completed in less than three months, and we flew back down in March 2010 to close on it. We intended to use this house as our winter getaway for the months of January, February, and March. We were snowbirds for a few years and took up the game of pickleball seriously during this time. I became an instructor for The Villages to introduce new people to the game. When we traveled back to Connecticut for the summer, there was no place to play, so Brenda and I became ambassadors for the USA Pickleball Association, and we introduced the new game to the towns of Manchester and Glastonbury, Connecticut. Of course, this was self-serving because now we would have a place to play while up north. One day, while playing in the parking lot of a senior center in Glastonbury with a temporary net and chalk lines on the pavement, a new fellow walked up to me. He said, "I know you. You were my pickleball instructor in Florida!" Dave Pudlo and his wife, Ann Marie, became good friends of ours and we keep in touch on a regular basis. Over the years we have made many good friends playing this sport.

I taught pickleball in The Villages for seven years and we play daily with a number of groups. Brenda has become so proficient at it that I nicknamed her "The Hammer" because of her powerful hits. We have encouraged many couples to come to The Villages, and some of them have bought into the lifestyle here. Pickleball has become the fastest-growing sport in the nation, with celebrities and professional athletes taking up the sport. You can now watch games on ESPN and YouTube. The Villages has become the mecca of pickleball, with over 230 courts available year-round. We love the lifestyle and will continue the game as long as our bodies allow. We have friends in their 80s and 90s who are still playing at a high level. In fact, we just came back from a tournament where our 90-year-old friend, Ernie Incorvati, and his fellow competitor, Rich Brend, competed. They won the best of three games and came home with a gold medal. How cool is that?

FRIENDS

My dad was a wise guy. Not in the sense of being a "smart ass," but rather in the wisdom that he shared with me from time to time. One of his most memorable stories was when he told me, "If you want to know how many REAL friends you have in this world, just ask them to borrow a large sum of money." That large sum of money may have been $100 sixty years ago, but it might be $1,000 or more in today's economy. I have never tested the theory, but I've always kept it in mind when deciding who my real friends might be. Of course, it goes without saying that my best friend is my wife, Brenda. In a way, I have tested the 'borrow money' concept from her. Any large sums of money that might be spent for, let's say, home improvement items, are discussed in detail before pulling the trigger. One sneaky exception was the birthday card that Brenda gave me recently. It had three boxes to check off.

Well, I couldn't make up my mind, so I checked off all three boxes! As it turns out, Brenda must be a super good friend because she agreed to all three choices. The budget could handle it, so we purchased the 65" OLED TV, bought a new 2022 Yamaha golf cart, and I got my dream $3,000 flight doing aerobatics in The Little Witch, a P51D Mustang based at Kissimmee Gateway Airport. Life is good.

My other 'best friends' were, of course, my mom and dad. They financed my formal education for me to become an engineer and allowed me to earn a good living for which I will always be grateful. Brenda's mom and dad also gifted us $1,000 to make some improvements to our home in Manchester, Connecticut, so they are definitely near the top of my 'best friend' list. Brenda and I must be on our children's 'best friend' list because we have financed education, house down payments, and home improvement projects to help them out over the years. Hopefully, they will do the same for their children someday.

We lived most of our working lives in the town of Manchester, Connecticut. With relatives nearby and in Massachusetts, you'd think that between them, work acquaintances, and neighbors, we'd have lots of good friends. I'm guessing that we could lean on some of them if we needed to borrow money, but I'd bet I could count the reliable ones on the fingers of one hand. New Englanders tend to be a little cold and standoffish for whatever reason. Maybe it's the long, cold winters. It seems that no one gets really close in a friendship. We have relatives who no longer talk to us because of either jealousy or "he said/she said" comments behind our backs. Life is too short to be like that, but such is the pettiness of some people.

Fast forward to retirement in Florida. It's a whole 'nother world down here. We have made so many friends in our neighborhood and the various social groups that we belong to. We have our Connecticut friends who moved here both before and after us. We have snowbird friends who we mingle with on the pickleball courts and stay in touch with the rest of the year. My favorite story is when we first came to The Villages many years ago. Brenda and I were at a pickleball court practicing in the afternoon. Another couple from Vermont showed up to practice, but they were new to the game. They seemed like a loving couple, so we struck up a conversation with them, practiced together, and played a few games. It was like we had known these people all our lives because we went out to dinner with them that first evening. We have become best friends with Chris and Pat Beltrami. Maybe someday I will test the 'real friend' theory and ask to borrow $1,000 from them. I'm betting the answer would be "yes." And I'd also bet that I would get a positive response from many of the other folks that we now call friends. That's just the way it is living in The Villages and "America's Friendliest Hometown." Goodbye New England, hello Southern hospitality!

Thanks, Dad, for passing along your "real friend" wisdom to me. I will share with our children and grandchildren. The lesson is timeless.

Horses

I've always loved horses. I especially like it when I see a foal that has just been born. It amazes me that before too long, they are attempting to stand up and, within a few days, are running around with Mamma. Living in central Florida, we are near the horse capital of the world, Ocala. They recently built the World Equestrian Center in Ocala, a wonderful destination. The hotel on the property is beautiful and the lobby is decorated in a grand way. The main show arena is located in front of the hotel with stadium seating on three sides. There is a bronze statue of a horse in front of the stadium. It is of a horse by the name of Sergeant Reckless. The mare served with a marine division during the Korean War, carried ammunition to the front lines, as well as transported wounded soldiers to safety. She was wounded twice and received two Purple Heart awards. She was considered a hero. A best-selling book has been written about Sgt. Reckless. I purchased the book, read it, and shared it with my friends. It is a wonderful, true story. The Center also has a series of large barns at the rear of the property that are used for various events, including car shows and auctions. We have attended a draft horse competition there as well as an American cowboy quarter horse competition. Just beautiful to watch.

Any discussion about horses could not be told without mentioning our daughter, Kimberly. She has always been a strong-willed girl who perseveres in all that she does. At an early age, she became a state and national champion in the sport of BMX bicycle racing. She has won trophies that were bigger than she was at the time. At the tender age of thirteen, she could beat most boys her age. She was awesome to watch. It wasn't long before she got her first job at a local doughnut shop and started to save money. She bought her first car on her own at sixteen and it wasn't long after that she bought, unbeknownst to us, a horse. She kept Quest at a local horse barn and rode almost every day. There must be a lot of dynamics with girls of differing personalities at a barn because Quest got moved several times in the coming years. Kimberly competed in various horse shows; it wasn't long before she got into hunter/jumper competition.

Kim was now boarding Quest at a farm in Bolton, Connecticut. We visited one day with my wife, Brenda, and her mom and dad. Brenda's dad, Joe, was a daredevil who knew no fear. He was in his 70s at the time and asked to ride Quest. As they trotted around the indoor arena, Joe urged the horse to go faster and faster. Brenda's mom was getting worried. She knew what Joe was capable of. They built up speed at the other end of the arena and headed for a big jump. Oh, no! Were Joe and Quest actually going to attempt to clear the obstacle? The answer is "yes." Up and over they went, effortlessly clearing the jump. I don't think Joe had ever ridden a horse in his lifetime but, like I said, he knew no fear.

Kim went on to own another horse, Windsong, and most recently, Vegas, who is of the Morgan breed. She's cracked a couple of helmets along the way from falling off horses, and she's dislocated a shoulder at least once that we know of. I guess when you are into horses, it's not a matter of 'if' but 'when' you will end up on the ground. Kimberly still owns Vegas but doesn't ride as often as she once did. She is a busy girl who recently earned a master's degree in education. We urged her from an early age to become a veterinarian, but that, for some reason, was not in the cards. She certainly had the aptitude to become one. She was always a whiz kid in math, science, and chemistry. She's our little smart-ass daughter!

Living in horse country in Florida is delightful. Expansive farms are everywhere. We recently took a tour of a Gypsy Vanner horse farm in Ocala. These horses are smaller versions of draft horses like Clydesdale, Percheron, Belgian and Friesian breeds. They were brought to the United States from Europe, where they were bred to pull Gypsy wagons or caravans. They are like painted ponies with long manes, feathered hocks, and long, free-flowing tails. Their temperament is serene and engaging. Such beautiful animals. During a tour of the farm, we learned that a Gypsy Vanner mare can only produce one offspring a year. To increase the number of foals, a veterinarian impregnates the mare. After 15 weeks, the embryo is removed and placed in a surrogate mare to carry it to full term. It is a very interesting breeding technique. It just goes to prove that you never stop learning.

We have a number of friends who own horses and ride often. One lady has trained her horse to compete in dressage which translates to "training" in French. This sport involves the execution of precise movements of the horse in response to barely perceptible signals from its rider. Beautiful to watch. Another friend owns a local tree nursery and also has a large horse farm in Ocala. Her favorite horse is a thoroughbred that retired from racing. Wendy rides with an inflatable vest (equestrian airbag), which activates if you fall off the horse. Probably a good idea for older riders. I have another friend who has retired to Oklahoma and breeds quarter horses. Apparently, they are one of the most popular and versatile breeds in the world. They can adapt to racing, trail riding, reining, dressage, jumping, and so much more. I love to watch them in "cutting" events for culling a steer from the rest of the herd. These horses are so athletic. And, of course, there are the Morgan horses like our daughter owns. These horses were bred on a neighboring farm when I was a kid. They were trained for carriage events.

I've never been tempted to own a horse, even as beautiful as they are. In my experience, they are so fragile for a large animal in that they are susceptible to injury and digestive problems. I don't know how horses survive in the wild. To properly take care of them, you have vet fees, boarding costs, farrier costs for shoeing, and feed and grain. And last but not least, mucking their stalls is always a fun chore. Then, there is the cost of "tack." The two basic types of saddles are English and Western. I have always liked the look and style of Western. As the saying goes, with Western, you can hang on to the saddle horn with one hand and hold a beer in the other! Just saying.

Our daughter, Kimberly, always loved horses. She had owned several of them over the years and liked to compete in the hunter/jumper class at shows. She has the cracked helmets and shoulder injuries to prove it! This picture is of her and Vegas going over a small jump. Just look at the intensity in her face. That's my girl.

BIKES

Most of us learned how to ride bicycles when we were kids. I can't remember how old I was when I got my first bike, but I don't think it had the obligatory training wheels. I just kept falling off until I got tired of getting banged up and eventually found my balance. I'm pretty sure my first bike or bikes were used hand-me-downs. At some point in time, I got a new bicycle from the local bike shop, and I was in seventh heaven. It was like somebody had given me a brand-new car. I don't even remember what the occasion was so I'm thinking I must have done something right or had been an exceptionally good kid to receive such a prize. My parents were shop workers and didn't earn a lot of money, so this gift was pretty extravagant in those early days. As I became older I eventually outgrew the bicycle stage of my life and moved on to cars when I turned sixteen.

We gave both of our kids the opportunity to ride a bicycle at an early age. As I recall, it didn't take them long to learn and they pretty much did it on their own. They were 'naturals.' One memory is of our daughter. At the early age of three or four, she started riding down a gentle slope in our backyard. I don't think she even had training wheels. If she fell, the grass offered a soft landing. Pretty smart. She eventually graduated to riding on the street. Another thing that sticks in my memory is our son when he was about four years old. We had training wheels on his bicycle, then took them off, and then put them back on again after a couple of failed attempts to go without the extra wheels. As I was leaving for work one morning, I had a talk with him. I showed him how to take the training wheels off and left him the tools to accomplish the task. Later that day I got a call from my wife. She said, "Brett took the training wheels off and he is determined to ride his bike without them. He will be successfully riding on two wheels by the time you come home." She was right. He learned to ride that day and never looked back. Both of our children went on to compete in dirt track Bicycle Motocross (BMX) racing on a state and national level. No more training wheels were required!

I hadn't ridden a bicycle in a long time, but as they say, "Riding a bike is something you never forget." They also say, "It's so easy; it's like falling off a bike!" I'm not sure I like that analogy because it may be easy to fall off a bike, but I recollect that it hurts like hell when you do. In retirement, we took up bike riding again. We bought a couple of new 24-speed bikes from our local shop along with the obligatory helmets. And, no, we didn't require training wheels at this stage of our lives! Most serious accidents result in head injuries, so we purchased some good helmets to protect our "coconuts." Besides riding locally in our community for a little exercise, we were invited to join others in our neighborhood to do some off-campus rides, which usually included brunch or lunch. During one of these rides, one of our experienced riders slid on some loose sand and fell on the pavement. She was knocked unconscious, but the cracked helmet prevented a more serious injury. If you are going to ride a bicycle, take it from us and invest in good equipment. It could save your life. We still ride our bikes from time to time. I'm thinking of getting a trailer hitch for our SUV and a bike rack so we can venture out to more riding trails. There are a lot of them in Florida. The Santos Trail in Marion County provides 80 miles of paved and unpaved routes. It's called the Cross Florida Greenway. The Withlacoochee State Trail in Inverness is another great place to ride. It is a 46-mile-long former rail line with gentle inclines which makes it easy for novice riders like us. There are hundreds of miles of bike trails in Florida to take advantage of and we are just now discovering a few of them.

There are some serious bike riders in our area of Florida. Some of them will bike 50 or 60 miles in a day. I'm good with less than ten, thank you very much! It is better to ride in groups because that makes the cyclists more visible to motorists. We have some very dear friends who were riding along one of the boulevards in our retirement community. Jessica and Rob were out for a morning ride, which they did quite frequently. They were experienced riders but that didn't make a difference because they were hit by an older lady driving a white Mercedes. She hit Jessica first and then Rob, knocking them both to the ground. The lady driver pulled over, got out of her car, took a look at the couple lying on the ground, got back into her car, and took off. That was her big mistake. Another vehicle stopped, called 911, and summoned medical help. Now, a couple of years after the accident, Rob and Jessica are still feeling the effects of getting hit by that car. Jessica, sadly, will probably never fully recover. The lady driver? Her first big mistake was leaving the scene of the accident. Her next mistake was having the car taken far away to Gainesville, Florida for repairs. She was eventually identified and prosecuted. She tried to use her 80+ age as a defense, but the judge would not hear of it. She knew better than to leave the scene of the accident and ended up in jail. The justice system works… sometimes.

E-bikes are the latest rage. We have not ridden one yet, but we have plenty of friends who do have them. You can ride an e-bike as a regular bicycle but then have the option of using a battery-operated motorized assist to go faster with less effort. They can be dangerous, especially for older people. One friend was gazing at golfers on a nearby putting green while driving his e-bike. He hit the curb and took a tumble onto the pavement. No broken bones were incurred, but the black and blue marks all over his body were a testament to what can happen if you are not attentive to keeping your eyes on the road. We are not ready for e-bikes yet, but that's not to say there might be one in the future. As the saying goes, you never forget how to ride a bike.

CLUBS

While we were still working and raising a family, we didn't have too many activities outside of home and work. My wife Brenda was, however, involved with the Manchester Junior Women's Club, which raised money for school scholarships and charities. It was a way to socialize with other women her age and give back to the community that we lived in. I belonged to the Manchester Coon and Fox Club because, at the time, I had a dog and was actively hunting. Our dog was named Sir Bentley of Coventry. He was a registered English Springer Spaniel. I believe everyone should be blessed with at least one good dog in their lifetime, and Bentley was mine. I shot a lot of birds over that dog, the first of which was when he was only five months old. The club also had a trap shooting range which I competed at from time to time. During bird season in the fall of the year, the club stocked pheasants in various locations around the property. One club member (we'll call him Butch) was always known to try to be the first one into a certain area of the property at sunrise, so the bird stocking committee thought it might be funny to put a couple of chickens in this area. Wouldn't you know it, on the first day of hunting season, Butch ran to be the first one into his favorite area. It wasn't long before two shotgun blasts were heard, and not long after Butch was done hunting for the day. When asked if he got anything, he replied that he got a couple of pheasants. The word got around, and everyone knew that he'd shot a couple of chickens on the ground. It was the talk of the club for months afterward. You can't make up this kind of humor!

Our son Brett and I were involved with archery shooting for a while, but then I gravitated to pistol shooting at a local range. Metropolitan Shooters Incorporated (MSI) was an indoor club located nearby in one of the buildings of the old, abandoned Nike missile site. I got involved in competition shooting at this range, served as Vice President for two years and President for another two years. I also was involved in teaching concealed carry permit classes and became an NRA-certified instructor. That was thirty years ago, and I still teach to this day. I have taught more than 1,000 students how to safely handle a handgun and have taught most of our neighbors in Florida. We are a well-armed community. Don't mess with us!

Because of my love for old cars and hot rods, I had a lot of friends who belonged to the Connecticut Street Rod Association. Many of these people became lifelong friends, and they helped me immensely while building several hot rods. When we retired to The Villages, Florida, we became involved in a plethora of activities. As it turns out, there are almost 3,000 clubs to choose from through the Residents Lifestyles programs. As a resident you can pick and choose what you want to get involved in, but you couldn't possibly have enough time to do them all. If you choose not to get involved in any of the clubs, that is a personal choice. I like to say that if you get bored living here, you must be a boring person. Just saying. We joined the Villages Convertible Club because of the BMW convertible that Brenda owns. We have gone on many tours with this group, and Brenda even got to do a few laps at the Daytona Motor Speedway. I urged Brenda to speed up to 100 mph on the straightaway, but she was a little reluctant to do so. Maybe she'll put the pedal to the metal on the next visit. We also belonged to the Straight Shooters Gun Club which made us eligible for discounts at the new Shooter's World indoor range nearby. We've spent many enjoyable hours there shooting with friends. Brenda has her own gun. You don't wanna mess with mama!

We belong to the Amigo's Sports Club. This club is very active and donates a lot of money to charity at Christmas and provides manpower to Habitat for Humanity. They also hold a dance each month featuring top-notch entertainment. We have made so many good friends through this club. And, of course, there are the many pickleball groups that we play with daily. Good fun, exercise, laughs, fresh air, and sunshine. It doesn't get any better than that. We play six times a week. The Villages Vintage Car Club is another organization I joined for a time to be able to get access to the monthly car show at Spanish Springs. I have brought my 1930 Ford roadster and 1932 Ford coupe there on numerous occasions. Since I still fly radio-controlled airplanes, I am a member of The Villages E-fliers. This club is dedicated to flying only electric-powered aircraft, which are clean and quiet. Nice technology.

I studied the online list of those 3,000 clubs and was

amazed to find a huge variety to choose from. They have clubs for bands, bicycles, billiards, boats, bridge, bunco, crafts, dance, exercise, mah-jongg, music, Parkinson's support, veterans, women doctors, yoga, and Zumba, just to name a few. If you play cards there are 275 groups just for that. If you like cats, how about the cat crazy club? We had a friend who was involved in the clown ally club. We went to a clown ally get-together one time, and I got talking with a gentleman who was all dressed up in his clown outfit. It turns out that he was a WWII fighter pilot. You meet the most interesting people in retirement. They have over 30 clubs for AA support. If you live in The Villages, there is a lot of drinking that goes on and, hence, AA! Every time I purchase an item in a store, I ask for either the senior, AAA, or AA discounts! A lot of retirees are overweight, so there is a solution for that as well ... the Over-eaters Anonymous group, of course. And you can follow up with the walk away the pounds groups, of which there are more than ninety. Is your name Elaine? The 'Elaine Is Our Name' club is just for you then.

As you can see, if you are bored in The Villages during retirement, the conclusion would be that you are a boring person. We often laugh at what we might be doing back in Connecticut during retirement, especially in the winter. The answer always is ... we'd be sitting in front of the fireplace, watching TV. We have friends and relatives up north who made the decision to stay there. They have no idea what they are missing out on here in the land of Dixie! Come on down!

TRAVEL

We are not world travelers by any stretch of the imagination. We have friends who travel all over the world. Dubai, Indonesia, China, South America, African safaris, Europe. Some friends of ours go on one or more cruises every year. My wife, Brenda, and I have been on exactly three cruises. The first one was on Norwegian Cruise Lines (NCL) to the Eastern Caribbean. Our ship was the Norway which was an older ship but had been recently refurbished. Not too many years later, the ship was sold for scrap and disassembled in an Indian port. The theme of that cruise was devoted to country music. We met some popular country singers of the day and danced to their latest hit songs. It was a good time with good friends. My first impression of the Caribbean is the beauty of the water. It is clear and made up of many shades of blue and green. Beautiful. It was an eye-opener when we went ashore on the first island. Next to the dock was a fisherman chopping the heads off his morning catch. It quickly became crystal clear that there were poor people on these islands and rich people, but no middle class. These islands are devastated almost annually by late summer and early fall hurricanes. The rich get all of the materials and labor to rebuild first. In the poorer neighborhoods, you can see almost every roof of every shack covered in blue tarps. This scene was repeated at each port of call. Sad.

Our second cruise was to the western Caribbean on one of the biggest ships in the Royal Caribbean fleet, the Oasis of the Seas. It was a beautiful ship. We never felt the rough seas and 70 mph winds on our first night at sea. After a stop in Nassau on the Bahamian island of New Providence to drop off a sick passenger, we headed to Labadie, Haiti. We felt adventurous, so we booked a boat tour to a secluded beach. We tried snorkeling, which we always wanted to do, but the equipment was not very good so we gave up on that and just swam. During a tour of a nearby village, we noted that the 'latrine' was spilling its effluent down the hillside and into the very waters we were just swimming in! I'm sure this was no biggie to the local people, but it was repulsive to us. As of this writing, Haiti has been overtaken by gangs. Crime is rampant and a travel ban is in effect. The Royal Caribbean Resort on Labadie is closed to tourists. It might be some time before this country is safe to travel to again. I feel bad for the people of Haiti because most, if not all, of their tourist dollars have been shut off. The other islands and ports in Mexico that we visited were just more of the same. Vendors and beggars in Mexico were overly pushy. We couldn't wait to get back on the ship!

Our third cruise was, again, to the Eastern Caribbean, but this time we went with a crazy group from the Amigos Sports Club that we belong to. The NCL ship, Encore, was big and beautiful. Our ports of call were in the Dominican Republic,

St. Thomas, and Tortola. We liked St. Thomas so much that we flew there for a week the following year on the occasion of our 54th wedding anniversary. A stop at Stirrup Cay in the Bahamas on the way back to Port Canaveral was very peaceful and relaxing. Our impression of the places we have seen in the Caribbean and the Bahamas is that they are very pretty, but they are basically tourist traps. See one and you've seen them all. I'm not saying we will never go on another cruise, but it might be a while before we do. After five days on a cruise ship, we are ready to go home. We are like Dorothy, clicking our heels and pronouncing, "There's no place like home. There's no place like home." We are definitely not world travelers.

There are so many places to go and things to see right here in the good old USA. We will probably just stay a little closer to home from now on. We recently looked into a music city tour with a travel agency. The itinerary would have taken us to New Orleans, Memphis, and Nashville and it was expensive. We finally decided to just do the trip in our own car. The first stop was New Orleans. I had booked us into an old hotel in the French Quarter. It was beautiful, recently renovated and our room overlooked the Mississippi River waterfront. The bartender at the hotel mixed a mean Hurricane so we visited that bar more than once! Just saying. We took a mule-drawn carriage ride around the historic district. Mules are used instead of horses because they are more tolerant of the heat and humidity. One evening, we boarded a stern-wheeler river boat for a wonderful dining and music experience. We visited the WWII museum which was spectacular. Another evening, we strolled around the French Quarter and stopped at the Balcony Music Club when we heard the band playing our favorite kind of music. We couldn't resist going in and dancing the East Coast

Swing. For some reason, we were the only couple dancing, so people started video recording us! They said, "You're going to be on Facebook and YouTube!" We never did find the videos of us, but this was certainly a very memorable, once-in-a-lifetime evening to remember.

Then, it was off to Memphis. We stayed at the Graceland Hotel and took a VIP tour of Elvis Presley's home and museum. A local girl accompanied us on the tour. She was very knowledgeable and explained exhibits to us that we otherwise would have walked right by. I was not a huge fan of Elvis when I was growing up, probably because he seemed a little radical to me at the time. Little did I realize how talented this guy was and I've come to realize this in my old age. There was one wall in the museum that was covered with awards that he had received during his lifetime, including gold and platinum records. Ironically, my parents actually liked Elvis, especially his recording of "Love Me Tender." They must have recognized his talent and overlooked his "gyrations." I didn't appreciate him at the time.

Brenda and I travel occasionally with the Convertible Club of The Villages. We have been to Georgia, the Daytona Speedway, the Stetson Museum, and many other venues. Brenda got to drive her BMW convertible around the track at the Speedway several times. I urged her to put the pedal to the metal on the straightaway, but I couldn't persuade her to hit 100mph. Maybe next time. One of my favorite events of the year is the annual fly-in at Loves Landing in Weirsdale, Florida. This is an airport community and everyone who lives there has a hangar next to their home. All kinds of aircraft fly in, including biplanes, antique, home-built, and experimental airplanes.

We've attended this event three years in a row. Brenda just puts up with it. Me? I'm in heaven.

So, to repeat, we are not world travelers. We have visited West Virginia a couple of times recently and gone to the Arc Encounter in Williamstown, Kentucky. We tend to stay closer to home in our old age. Maybe we will drive down to the Florida Keys or Anna Maria Island for our 55th wedding anniversary. There are lots of options. We wish safe travels to all our friends venturing off to exotic places. There certainly is something for everybody.

Our ship, Norwegian Cruise Line ENCORE in port at St. Thomas, USVI. The picture was taken by a friend, Kathy Morrissette, from a high vantage point. Kathy and her husband own Tickles Dockside Pub in one of the marinas nearby. We spent a week in St. Thomas last year on the occasion of our 54th wedding anniversary. The water has more shades of blue than you can count! Just beautiful.

St. Thomas

As I have previously stated, we are not world travelers. We have no desire to go to Europe, China, or Abu Dhabi. Many of our friends do love to travel, though, and some are gone for long periods of time. It is expensive to travel. We have the money but not the desire to go to foreign countries. From the limited business travel I have done, I have always found it was good to get back home with the realization that we 'have it made' here in the good old USA. "There's no place like home," as Dorothy stated in The Wizard of Oz. Domestically, there are a number of states that I have not yet been to but would like to visit someday. Alaska and Hawaii are on the list, as well as some of the upper mid-west states like Idaho, Montana, the Dakotas, and Nebraska. As we get older, we realize that traveling can be dangerous on the nation's highways and byways. There is so much more traffic now than when we were younger and they are going much faster. We travel a steady 80mph on good highways, but it's not fast enough for some people who end up passing us. Since the COVID-19 pandemic, there are so many more trucks on the road and it seems like they just love to hog the passing lane for some reason. Maybe it's just to annoy non-commercial vehicles. So often, an eighteen-wheeler will pull out to pass another truck and then just keep pace with it. I swear they do it to piss off the general public. With the growth of Amazon, it is now so easy to order something online and have it delivered the very next day. This adds to the truck traffic. We see Amazon, FedEx, and UPS vehicles going up and down our neighborhood streets all the time. Some of them go too fast, probably trying to stay on schedule. Years ago, we had a delivery truck smash into the back of our family car. The rear window was demolished and all the glass ended up hitting our daughter in the back seat. Thankfully, no one got seriously hurt. The driver admitted he was looking at his on-board computer and not watching the road in front of him.

We have traveled on several cruises to the Caribbean and the Bahamas. The islands are beautiful, but after seven days, we are ready to get back home. We did like St. Thomas, though, and had fun with our gang from The Villages. One highlight was going for a boat ride on the Screamin' Eagle jet boat. We were warned that we would get wet on this ride, so we all wore bathing suits. And get wet we did! There was not a dry seat anywhere on this boat. What a thrill. For our 54th wedding anniversary, we flew back to St. Thomas for a week and stayed in a very nice Airbnb condo overlooking the Caribbean Sea. The view from our balcony was to die for. I never realized there could be so many shades of blue water! We rented a jeep from a local business and quickly found out that you must drive on the left side of the road in St. Thomas! Let's just say it took a little getting used to. We were warned by people who frequented the island to be cautious of oncoming traffic. The roads are hilly and extremely narrow. We were told that many vehicles were missing their right-side mirrors because of the narrow roads, and this turned out to be true. Public transportation is so good there that we really didn't need to rent a vehicle. Local buses and taxis are everywhere but I still liked the convenience of having a vehicle at our disposal.

One of our pickleball friends, Kathy Morrissette, owns Tickles Dockside Pub at a marina in St. Thomas. Of course, we had to visit the pub and try a Bushwacker, the island's signature drink. The drink was invented in 1975 at the Ships Store, Sapphire Pub, in the village where we stayed. I'll describe the drink as a tasty concoction of alcohol (rum), not unlike a Hurricane, which is famous in New Orleans. We did some snorkeling at the local Sapphire beach and had our anniversary dinner at the restaurant there. The next day, we drove to Lindquist Beach to do some more snorkeling. The parking lot was at the entrance, so I dropped Brenda off at the beach and went back to park the Jeep. When I hiked back to the beach and settled in, it was time to jump into the water for some swimming and snorkeling. What I failed to do was remove the Jeep remote entry key from my bathing suit pocket! Key fobs apparently don't like salt water or any kind of water, for that matter. After taking the fob apart and drying it out as best I could, I determined that it was definitely ruined. Luckily, I was able to gain entry to our vehicle, start the engine and drive to the rental place for a replacement key. I'll have to be more careful in the future. Note to self: Remove electronic key from bathing suit pocket prior to entering water.

We took the ferry to St. John for a day trip. We had lunch there and struck up a conversation with a local boat captain who had beached his small boat so his wife and passengers could get lunch and do a little shopping. He was an interesting guy who was originally from the Midwest but was now living on the islands and working remotely from home. As we were preparing to return to the ferry boat, I realized I did not have my Visa card on me! I must have left it on the table where we had lunch. I approached the bartender and told her of my dilemma. She looked through a stack of credit cards that was the size of a double deck of playing cards but didn't find mine. A waitress searched another stack of cards and came up with our card! We got lucky.

On our return flight to Orlando, we again flew Spirit Airlines. We were warned that the last half hour of the flight would be rough. It was probably in the top ten of the roughest flights I had ever experienced. We landed and lived to tell about it. Actually, it was a great landing because they could use the airplane over again! Just saying. It was nice to get back to 'home, sweet home.'

COVID

Looking back in history, my mother told me of an event in 1918. It was Spanish flu and was thought to have been brought back from Europe by soldiers returning from WWI (1914-1918). My mother, born in 1907, was eleven years old at the time. Her older brother, Edwin, was about eighteen and had been drafted into the army. Edwin, who would have been an uncle of mine, contracted the flu before entering the service. He died at home after about two weeks of suffering. His skin color turned black upon his demise, which may be the reason this influenza was sometimes referred to as the black plague. Out of fear of contracting the flu, most people did not attend funerals or burials, which is understandable. Hearses going up and down the streets were a common sight. This strain of influenza lingered until 1920.

It has been prophesied that every one-hundred years or so there will be a major pandemic. So, right on schedule, COVID-19 hit us in 2019. This pandemic likely started with the release of a pathogen from Wuhan Wangrui Laboratory in China. The release may have been a mistake, but it may have also been intentional. We will never know for sure, but by the beginning of 2020, COVID-19 was spreading to the entire world. With President Trump in office, international flights from China to the United States were almost immediately cut off. Our pharmaceutical companies were given the green light to fast-track a vaccine to combat the flu. Surgical masks were in high demand. They flew off the shelves and became back-ordered online. We obtained our first masks from, ironically, our eyeglass store, Hindsight. One of the technicians who worked there was at the curb of the shopping center handing out masks. I gratefully accepted a couple of them.

When the new flu shots became available, it was a panic to try to get them. People were making appointments wherever they could. Some of our neighbors and friends drove a hundred miles or more to receive them. I was able to get my vaccine locally, but for Brenda, we had to drive 30 miles to a pharmacy in Ocala, Florida where we could finally get an appointment. After the first shot, we were encouraged by our doctors to get the second shot as soon as it became available. I had no reaction to either of these vaccines, but Brenda developed a rash all over her face and had to see her dermatologist to clear the outbreak. Our bodies are chemically unique and react in different ways to injections. We never had a reaction to flu shots, which we got annually, but this COVID-19 shot was made up of a cocktail of drugs that our bodies were not used to. At our doctor's urging, we eventually went for one more booster shot. Of course, Brenda broke out again. We both vowed that that was the last time we would ever take a vaccine that was government-recommended for COVID. And we didn't.

Having taken the COVID vaccinations and yielded to the precautionary wearing of masks, we still contracted COVID-19. We initially tested positive using home test kits provided by the government free of cost. The kits were, ironically, made in China. What is suspiciously wrong with this picture? The drug Paxlovid was prescribed, and a week later, we were in recovery. We surmise that we might have had a worse case of this flu if we had not gotten the two COVID shots and a booster. Hydroxychloroquine was another drug that we had on hand if necessary. Our doctors would not prescribe it for us, but we could purchase it online from a clinic in New Jersey. This drug was commonly used to combat malaria and apparently, was effective against COVID too.

After the initial year of panic, we decided collectively to just go on with our lives as usual. There is some humor associated with such a devastating sickness, though. We saw someone driving a motorcycle with a mask on. Really? Hell, you're out in the fresh air. Take the damn mask off! We've seen people on the pickleball court wearing a mask while playing in really hot weather. I would die from not being able to breathe! All kidding aside, though, a lot of people died from this form of influenza. A lot of mistakes were made by the government. COVID affected older adults much worse than children. On the national level, Dr. Fauci became the leading expert on combating the disease. Ironically, he was associated with the Chinese Wuhan lab, which caused the problem to start with and he also was in bed with the pharmaceuticals developing and distributing the vaccine. I'm just guessing, but I'm willing to bet that he personally made millions of dollars from his involvement. On the state level, another bad actor was Governor

Cuomo of New York. He took sick older people out of New York City hospitals and nursing homes and distributed them to other facilities throughout the state, thereby spreading the disease. A Coast Guard medical ship was provided to the city, but they never used it! What a calamity of errors!

If there is one thing that I take away from the COVID experience, it's hygiene. Good hygiene habits will probably help avoid common colds, infections, common flu, and the like. A good friend, Bob Maxwell, really drove the point home for me. He said, "I'm 75 years old, and I've just now learned how to properly wash my hands!" We never worried too much about washing hands until COVID came along. I'm surprised we survived all these years without knowing that you need to scrub with hot, soapy water long enough to sing the Happy Birthday song ... twice. Geez, now I feel like a doctor prepping for surgery every time I wash my hands!

This was all a learning experience for me. I wonder if another worldwide pandemic will occur one hundred years from now. Guess I'll never know. I will be long gone. God bless future generations.

BIRDS

When we lived and worked in Connecticut, a sure sign of spring was the spotting of a Robin. "When the Red, Red, Robin Comes Bob, Bob, Bobbin' Along" was a popular tune written by Harry Woods in 1926. These birds had bright red breasts and were a pleasure to see after a long, cold winter. Of course, we had other birds that made it through the winter in New England, but the robin was a migratory species that was smart and headed south for the winter. You could always tell a robin's nest in the springtime because of the bright blue eggs. I'm not a bird-watching fanatic, but I could never ignore the presence of crows, red-tailed hawks, sparrows, chickadees, and woodpeckers, to name a few. During one of my morning hikes in the woods behind our house, I spotted a huge owl. He (or she) just stared me down and gave me a little "whoo the hell are you?" Nice to see. Anything avian refers to birds. The term 'aviator' comes from our winged friends. I just came to realize that from my research.

Living in Florida is a whole other world. We have lots of birds in Florida that are here all year long and some are really big, with wingspans of six feet or more. The sandhill crane comes to mind since we see them all year. Apparently, their main breeding ground is in, of all places, Nebraska along the Platte River. They do breed in Florida also and I can verify that from personal experience. Playing golf one warm spring day, we hit our second shot on a par 5 fairway, jumped into the golf cart, and proceeded down the paved path on our way to our balls. We passed a stand of palm trees with tall grass planted around the outcropping. Without warning, a pair of adult cranes attacked us as we passed near them. Why such behavior? They were protecting their newborn chicks that were hiding in the tall grass! At any other time of year, they will walk right up to you as they are feeding, or they will come in and land near you announcing their arrival with loud, honking sounds that can be heard a couple of miles away. Beautiful birds and always a delight to see... or hear! On a rather sad note, I was out and about in our car recently and I had to come to a stop because of a couple of cranes in the road. It is not unusual to see them casually crossing the road, so most people give them a wide berth. In this case, someone had hit one of the chicks and it was lying dead in the road. The adult birds stayed near the chick and didn't want to leave it behind. Some kind gentleman from a nearby house came out and mercifully removed the chick from the road. The saddened adults and their one remaining chick slowly left the area with their heads hanging low.

A few years ago, we witnessed the migration of a huge mass of robins from Florida. We don't see them too often, so this was an unusual sighting. They were obviously gathering up for their annual pilgrimage to the north. There were so many of them at times, it was like a dark cloud passing overhead, almost like a scene from the Alfred Hitchcock movie "The Birds!" In our backyard, we had several holly trees that, at the time, were loaded with red berries. The robins must have been hungry because they descended on those trees and noisily devoured all the berries in a matter of minutes. Holy shit! I had never seen anything quite like that before and nothing like that since. In a day or two, the 'clouds' of birds vanished from the area, and all was quiet again. Nature is a strange and beautiful thing. My dad used to tell me, "Birds of a feather flock together." His German version was "Birds mit ein fedder flock by demselves." Fatherly humor.

We have flocks of pelicans descend on us from time to time. It's fun to watch them work together in the local ponds to corral fish and then dive down to capture them for a quick lunch. The Anhinga, or snake bird, is interesting to watch as they dive in the ponds for fish. They cannot fly with wet wings, so you will see them on the shore spreading their wings to dry. Herons are another large species that are frequently seen in our area. The blue heron is my favorite. Egrets are also a common sight. They look like statues as they hunt for fish at the edge of ponds or mice in the tall grasses. I have seen them swallow a snake whole. I guess you'll eat anything if you are hungry enough. Snakes are fair game.

The White Ibis is another beautiful bird with long, curved bills. Have you ever seen a wood stork? They are the fabled big birds that deliver babies, right? They look beautiful in the air with their white body and black wing tips, but up close they are really ugly with wrinkled heads. I mean, disgustingly ugly. I wouldn't want one of them delivering my baby! Another bird we see on rare occasions is the swallow-tailed kite with its distinctive "V" shaped tail feathers. It's a real treat to see one in flight.

The state bird of Florida is the mockingbird. They are everywhere and are particularly noisy during mating season in the springtime. They have a variety of songs they can voice and are interesting to listen to. They start singing at four o'clock in the morning when they are active and get extremely feisty if you approach their nest. They will fight off any kind of human, animal, or bird intruder with gusto. The master-planned retirement community of The Villages has set aside large tracts of land for eagles to nest. Some of this land is shared with gopher turtles. Eagles can be seen from time to time, circling and looking for food. Their white heads and tail feathers are easily recognizable. Sometimes, they will even build nests on top of communication or high-power transmission towers. I've witnessed them grabbing big fish out of a pond next to the golf course. They are expert hunters. It's fun to watch osprey hover and then dive into a pond to snag a fish. We also have pink flamingos in southern Florida, but I have never spotted one in central Florida.

This story would not be complete without mentioning turkey vultures. They are birds that clean up the remains of dead creatures. They do not kill moving prey. They are ugly up close but beautiful to watch as they fly overhead, catching rising columns of warm air to high altitudes of several thousand feet or more... all without flapping their wings. Wildlife in Florida is like a menagerie and a constant reminder of the diverse creations of God—beautiful to behold in all their variations.

There are many kinds of birds in Florida. They flock here in droves during the winter months. One of our favorites is the Sandhill Crane which have wing spans of up to 6 ½ feet. These big birds are very comfortable being near people. They must not feel threatened by us. But don't get near them when they have their newly hatched chicks with them in the springtime. They get really defensive!

SNAKES

I hate snakes. The only good ones are dead ones. Serpentologists would surely disagree. They'd argue that snakes are part of the ecosystem and serve a purpose in the balance of nature. I'm sure there is some truth to that, but I still hate snakes. When I was a kid, we neighborhood boys caught a small snake and cut the head off with scissors. Watching the headless body wiggle for a long time was weirdly satisfying. It's like a chicken running around with its head cut off. I guess it was just something boys experiment with. After all, boys will be boys.

When I was a little older, I went fishing with some friends at a nearby farm pond. One of the older boys noticed a snake hanging over the water's edge, getting a drink. It was a big, black water snake about six feet long. New England didn't have water moccasins, so it probably wasn't poisonous. My friend snuck around behind the snake, grabbed it by the tail, and swung it around like a lasso. After a few twirls, he released it, and it went flying through the air. This was eerily amusing to me at the time.

Not too long after, I was hanging around a farm with friends. The boy who lived there brought us over to the pond on his property to do some fishing. As I was walking the shoreline path, I stopped abruptly when I saw a big black water snake coiled up on the path. I froze. I stood there for a moment staring at this big thing. He was looking at me also. I decided not to challenge him but when I turned around to head back along the path, another big black water snake emerged from a hole in the embankment and slowly slithered across the path. I was trapped. I did not like that feeling. Eventually, that snake made its way into the water and disappeared. As soon as he did that, I backtracked along the path and got the hell out of there. I never went back.

We had a neighborhood boy down the street who loved snakes. I saw him walking by the house one day with a big one he had caught. It was wrapped around his arm and body as he nonchalantly walked by. Really? You like snakes that much? Thank you very much, but not for me.

My next encounter with snakes was when I was working as a test engineer at the West Palm Beach Pratt & Whitney engine facility in Florida. I was in charge of running an experimental engine at the C10 test stand. I came into work one morning, greeted the test stand crew, went over to my desk, and opened my briefcase, which I left there overnight. As I opened it, a snake had been put in there and, as soon as I saw it, I slammed the lid closed. The snake was dead but still scared the shit out of me. I went for coffee and told the crew, "When I come back, that God damn snake better be gone." As the story goes, it was a pigmy rattlesnake that a crew member stepped on as he went out the door. It was sunning itself on the pavement. The guy jumped up and down as the snake struck at him until his foot finally came down on the snake's head. We had some laughs over this encounter in the coming days. On another morning, I arrived at the test stand, opened the door, and walked in to find all of the test stand crew sitting high up on the counters. What the hell is going on now? Apparently, a large poisonous snake had come in through the partially open door and slithered into hiding somewhere within the test stand. "Ummm, I'm going to the cafeteria to get another cup of coffee. I'll be back later... maybe." I did mention I hated snakes... right?

The lead test crew member liked to hunt. He told me of an incident that happened recently. They outfitted a jeep with a couple of seats mounted high in the rear. Their hunting dog worked the area before them, trying to sniff out wild pigs. A huge rattlesnake struck the dog and bit him in the neck. He got hit so hard it sounded like he was hit by a baseball bat. They killed the snake and got the dog to the vet as soon as possible. It was too late. The dog died.

So, here we are, living in retirement in Florida. We've had a couple of black racer snakes get onto our lanai and into the pool. One day, Brenda was swimming, and I was skimming surface debris with a net when I spotted a snake wiggling around in the pool. I called out to Brenda about it. That's all she had to hear. She was out of that pool like a porpoise! She didn't even use the stairs. Not too long after that, Brenda spotted another snake in the garage. I was having lunch, so I just raised the garage door, figuring he'd find his way out. After lunch, I checked the garage. No snake, so I lowered the door. The snake had somehow ridden the door into the up position and now almost fell on top of me as it flopped to the floor! I got a rake and escorted it onto the road. He must have known it was going to be his last day on Earth because he raised his head and shook his tail so violently it sounded like a rattlesnake. Of course, I killed him. Did I mention that I hate snakes? The only good ones are dead ones!

MUSIC

Most people die with their music still inside of them, or so I've heard. This could be true. There are a lot of nasty people out there who could surely use a big dose of soothing music. As a youngster growing up, my dad introduced my sister and me to music by teaching us how to play the trumpet. Our dad had played trumpet and cornet over the years with a variety of bands and orchestras. That is how he met our mother. Dad was playing at a town gazebo during a summer concert and my mother-to-be spotted him on the stage. She thought he was a good-looking young Italian man because of his dark, curly hair. Turns out he was German, just like her. They hit it off, and the rest is history. Is it too corny to say, "They made music together?"

Dad started teaching my sister and me when we became teenagers. We played in the school band and the occasional concert at the Clinton, Massachusetts town hall. We also played in church from time to time. At an Easter sunrise service, it was a little embarrassing when our trumpets froze up and we couldn't play one note. Dad had even coated the trumpet valves with kerosene to prevent freezing, but that didn't help. It was freaking cold that morning! Being German, my dad was like a military drill sergeant. He insisted on us learning everything with military precision, and when we didn't get it right, his raised voice let us know he was not pleased. Later, in my teens, I had had enough. Playing the trumpet was no longer fun, and I was more interested in the guitar, girls, and cars anyhow. So, I put down the trumpet and never picked it up again. Music has to be fun to be fully enjoyed. Plunking away on a guitar and doing a little singing was much more enjoyable to me.

As the years went on, I played the guitar from time to time but never really got serious about it. For a while, I took lessons from Bob Desjardins, my wife, Brenda's, cousin. I switched from acoustic to electric during this time. I bought my first really nice Fender American Standard Telecaster guitar and amplifier from Joe's Music Shop in Wallingford, Connecticut. This guitar was easy to play and I learned a lot from cousin Bob. Fast forward years later to our retirement in Florida. With more time on my hands, I switched back to acoustic, and with the urging of good friend Chris Beltrami, I came out of the closet, so to speak. I had never really played in front of a crowd other than family and friends, but Chris gave me the confidence to start playing before larger groups of people. Our singalongs with neighbors and friends became a popular pastime. It was a lot of fun, and since we provided free wine and beer, everyone had a good time. We'd tell people, "Please join in and sing along with us. If you can harmonize, all the better. If you are shy or sing off-key, just move your lips!" We had many great times hosting singalongs and I was improving my guitar picking.

When Brenda and I were first married, one of the popular artists at the time was Don Ho (his name would have a much different meaning today) from Hawaii. His hit song was Tiny Bubbles. For our sing-alongs, I bought a ukulele, learned the chord shapes, and sang this song. Another ukulele favorite was Over the Rainbow by Hawaiian artist Izzy Kamakawiwo'ole. We had some great get-togethers and even led a Christmas sing-along at a recreation center one year. Good fun. Good people.

Brenda and I both love music, so this is what led us to take up country dancing. Eventually, we bought cowboy boots and outfits and danced or took lessons four nights a week. We could be found practicing on our back deck, to the dismay of our kids. At one point, we had a repertoire of sixty dance routines. They were all choreographed to a specific song. The music made our feet move, just like the 2006 animated jukebox musical comedy film Happy Feet! When we retired to The Villages, Florida, we took up East Coast Swing dancing, which remains our favorite dance style. We don't like ballroom dancing. It is too formal for us. We are confident enough to dance in front of a crowd anytime the mood strikes us. When we hear a specific "beat," we instinctively know if we will do a cha-cha, two-step, or swing dance. On a trip to New Orleans, we danced to a band at the Balcony Music Club in the French Quarter. We were the only ones on the dance floor and were video recorded by some of the patrons. It was a beautiful memory. Music always gets our feet moving. We can be sitting in front of the TV and when a song comes on that we like, our feet start tapping to the beat of the tune. We are definitely not going to die with our music inside of us!

FOOD PANTRY

I'm not a religious person, but I do believe in God and I try to live each day as a good Christian. The golden rule, "Do unto others as you would have them do unto you," is something that everyone should live by. My wife, Brenda, goes to church every week. I don't remember her ever missing a service. During COVID-19, when churches were closed, she "attended service" online, and of course, she always gave her fair share of a monetary offering. She is devoted to making her weekly "sacrifice." Most recently, she decided to go to church every day during Lent and even gave up alcohol during that time which is a huge sacrifice for a retired person living in The Villages! I go to church with her on rare occasions. If we are traveling or on vacation, I have been known to accompany her to church. I get big points for this! One Easter service, I felt the need to go along with Brenda. The service lasted for almost three hours. The service included couples renewing their vows, baptisms, and some other special ceremonies which I cannot remember. What

I do remember is that I felt I had earned enough points to last me for a whole year!

We are surrounded by a number of good friends. When we share a meal, we always hold hands and say a prayer. I actually like doing that. It always gives me a good feeling. We are reminded by our friends from time to time to "shine our light." It is such a simple thing to do. Just smile and be pleasant to everyone you meet. One of my favorite opportunities to "shine" is when I am at the checkout counter of the grocery or department store. I always greet the person at the register with a cheerful "Well, hello there!" This simple greeting almost always gets a cheerful reply and usually opens up a smiling conversation. Such an easy thing to do. I'm sure there are a lot of grumpy old farts and people of all ages coming through those checkout lines, but this greeting is always a welcome gesture. I wish more people would learn to "shine their light."

I don't go to church often, but I do volunteer to work at the food pantry with Brenda for St. Vincent de Paul Catholic Church. The pantry is named Our Mother of Mercy. It's a simple obligation of an hour or two several times per month. Our morning starts with picking up donated food and essential items from the church and loading them into our SUV. After a short drive to the pantry, the items are unloaded, weighed, and sorted. There are usually a number of people on the team, which makes the task pretty easy. The more, the merrier. Busy hands are happy hands, so our hands are pretty happy while stocking the shelves. We have met so many nice people volunteering to do this work. We have been doing this for almost ten years. When we first started, one couple, Linda and Jim, were a little aggressive while directing us on what to do. So much so that I took offense and commented that I was retired and didn't need another boss directing my every move. Our relationship cooled with this couple until years later. We had just finished our work at the pantry and headed home. After an hour or so, we realized we had left a jacket there. We drove back to the pantry only to find that Linda and Jim were still there after everyone had left. They were diligently sorting items on the shelves so the next volunteers arriving would have everything perfectly arranged. They were going above and beyond what was expected of them when no one was watching. From that point on, I took a different view of this couple, apologized to them, and became a good friend. I get warm hugs now every time we meet. Funny how your perspective of people changes with time.

Not everything is flowers and roses in life. Some people are dealt a bad hand. We have friends whose spouses have died. Although never easy, it kind of goes with the demographics of the retirement community we are living in. You expect this in Florida in "God's waiting room," as one friend so aptly noted. You hate to see anybody suffering, as we recently witnessed with a friend suffering from ALS, Lou Gehrig's disease. This was so sad to watch and I'm not sure what I would have done in a similar situation. I might have chosen the "comfort option." We don't have a lot of choices when it comes to health. All we can do is keep volunteering, keep playing sports for as long as we can, and "shine our light" whenever possible. Finding God is comforting.

FAMILY

We have been blessed with two great kids, Kimberly and Brett. They both came from the same upbringing and are successful in their chosen paths in life, but their personalities differ in so many ways. Regardless, we love them both and pray for their health and happiness as they navigate the ups and downs of life.

Our daughter had four children. We spent a lot of time with our oldest granddaughter, Tuesday, because she lived with us for a time as a youngster. Her parents, Kimberly and Russ, never got married but they both truly loved this little girl. We spent a lot of time with this child and took her places we might not have gone if not for her. To name a few—the butterfly garden, dinosaur park, the life revealed exhibit in Hartford, steam train and boat ride in Essex, Connecticut were all visited with this little girl. Tuesday loved to read and I laugh at the notion that she read more books by the age of 15 than I have in my entire lifetime! Russ tragically died recently from an overdose. He was a good father and a genuinely nice guy, but he made some bad choices in life. Tuesday is a Vermont girl now and will probably continue her life up there in Bernie Sanders's land. Our thoughts and prayers are always with her.

Jared was born as the first child of Kimberly and Dave. As a baby, he developed a digestive problem that took him from a chubby, healthy kid to one who looked like he was a poster child for cancer. He could not keep anything down in his stomach and was losing weight, but smiled throughout the whole ordeal. Doctors at the children's hospitals in Newington and Hartford could not solve the problem. As a last resort and at the insistence of my wife, Brenda, we took him to a naturalistic doctor. This doctor put him on a special diet which included licorice, of all things. Within a short time, he responded to this treatment to our relief. Jared has grown up to be a physically strong young man and is now attending engineering school at the University of Massachusetts. Smart kid. Wonderful outcome.

Lacey was the next to be born and has always been a happy kid. I remember her big smile as she lay in her crib as a baby. What a delightful child. She had some early childhood symptoms of juvenile rheumatoid arthritis, which really concerned us. With medication and time, it appears that she has outgrown this disease and is in remission. Our hopes and prayers have been answered. Lacey is currently in high school and doing very well. Great kid.

Piper came along as a sort of surprise. Dave was unhappy about this news but just remember, it takes two to tango! Piper was so different from her siblings in body and mind. She had a rough time in school initially because of behavioral problems for whatever reason. With time and discipline, she slowly assimilated to her surroundings and is actually now getting good grades. This girl is a great athlete, has no fear on any stage, and I predict, she'll surprise us all by what she will accomplish in life. Just like our kids, these grandchildren are all different and unique in so many ways. God bless them all. I should mention at this time that after ten years of marriage, Kimberly and Dave separated and divorced. It has been a bitter custody battle ever since. Enter Steve Benoit who is a great guy and loves Kimberly and her kids. The children all cherish him. Kim and Steve married and are making a nice life together. We are so pleased with this happy ending. Now that Steve is an integral part of our family, we naturally consider his two children, Lindsay and Nathan, as our grandchildren too. We can brag to everyone that we have, not six, but eight, grandchildren!

Our son, Brett, and his wife, Maria have two boys, Mason and Braylon. We love our daughter-in-law, and we love her family in West Virginia. Beautiful people. Mason had some early childhood problems with allergies, so much so that it required intense therapy and medication. During one particularly bad night when he was struggling to breathe, he came down the hallway in the wee hours of the morning calling out "Mom, Dad, anybody?" Your heart has to go out to this kid as he battled this health problem. Good news. Mason has grown up to be a tall, handsome young man who is doing well in school and playing hockey at a very high level. Great parents, great outcome.

Next in line is Braylon. We weren't sure Brett and Maria would have another child after the health issues with Mason.

Maybe they were trying for a girl, but we will never know for sure. Braylon is a happy kid and again, so different from his brother. He is turning out to be a great student and a great athlete. He played baseball for a while but then turned his attention to basketball and football. He thrives in both sports but is amazing when throwing a football. This kid has an arm on him! He attended quarterback school for a couple of years and can hit receivers with uncanny accuracy. His hero is Jalen Hurts of the Philadelphia Eagles. Braylon is looking to become the quarterback for his high school football team. Maybe we'll see him on TV someday. Maybe he can get us good seats at his games in the VIP section. We love to see our kids and grandkids thrive in their lives and activities. I think we live vicariously through them.

Hopefully, there will be great-grandkids at some point. We look forward to this milestone and hope we are still active and healthy enough to know and enjoy them. God bless them all.

West Virginia

One of the first times we had been in the state of West Virginia was when our kids were bicycle motocross (BMX) racing at a national level. They had raced in upstate New York, Homestead, Florida, New Jersey, Alabama, Nashville, and everywhere in between. On our trip to the season-ending grand national race in Louisville, Kentucky we had an experience that could have ended in tragedy and one that I will never forget. We were traveling through the hills and tunnels of West Virginia with our van and trailer, climbing a steep grade in the passing lane. An eighteen-wheeler was coming in the other direction of the divided highway, gaining speed as it negotiated the hill. Our combined speeds were probably north of 120 mph. All of a sudden, I noticed something getting blown off the top of the truck's trailer. It was a piece of lumber that, for some reason, had been left on the roof. The piece of wood looked like a 2x8 and I estimate it was probably about eight feet long. I remember this chunk of wood spiraling through the air, almost in slow motion, and heading straight for us. I could not change lanes because a car was in the adjacent lane. All I could do was slam on the brakes and pray. Praying must have worked because that piece of lumber landed on the road in front of us, parallel to our vehicle, and slid under our van and trailer without making contact. We were very lucky, and we went on to have a successful trip without further incident. Welcome to West Virginia!

It would be many years later that we'd get back to the Mountain State. As it turns out, our son married a wonderful girl from Clendenin where her family still lives to this day. I call her our pretty Appalachian daughter-in-law. More recently, Brett and Maria purchased a 142-acre piece of property in that very town. It will be their destination for retirement. On the property stands a two-story house, a three-bay garage, a horse barn and a tractor with attachments, including a brush hog, of all things. There are trails leading up to the highest point on the property which consists of a number of acres of pastureland. It's just beautiful up there with views of the smokey valleys down below in all directions. God's country. We have been fortunate to visit Clendenin during the 4th of July celebrations for the last two years in a row. A private, huge, fireworks display is lit off at dusk on the top of the mountain and is a sight to behold. Maria's mother, brothers, and sister have taken our son under their wings and treated him like family. I think that people from West Virginia are perceived to be poorly educated and living in a "holler" somewhere back in the shadow of a mountain. And, while this may be somewhat true in some instances, there are smart, educated folks living there, too, like Maria's family. These are wonderful, hard-working people who make us feel at home just like family when we are visiting.

Deep in the woods, there are moonshine stills operating just like in the old days. It was illegal to produce moonshine during prohibition in the early 1900s, but now it is legal to make small batches. When Brett and Maria were married in a barn in Old Wethersfield, Connecticut, her mother and siblings brought gallons of 'white lightning' from home to be used as reception favors. The trip that normally takes eight hours actually took nine or ten hours traveling at the speed limit. They did not want to get pulled over by state troopers and found to be smuggling more than the legal limit of "hooch." It was a beautiful wedding and reception. People who had never before drunk 140 to 160-proof moonshine sampled it and found it to be a delightful stimulant for dancing. At one point, a jug cradled in an arm and hoisted to the lips was passed around a circle of dancers. Hilarious. The 'boys' showed me how potent moonshine burned with a blue flame. That was 'the good stuff.' Needless to say, everyone had a good time.

Meanwhile, when we were visiting Brett and Maria's property in West Virginia, we all pitched in to help work on the house and surrounding yard. I was commandeered to mow the pasture behind the horse barn with a riding tractor. No problem. I was up to the task. At some point, I pulled over next to the woods to relieve myself. I thought I was alone, but then heard a buzzing sound behind me. It was a drone that our son had brought along to scout the property for deer. Our grandson, Mason, was operating it and took a video of my private moment. That little shit! The video circulated among family and friends for quite some time thereafter. I gotta admit, it was pretty funny.

Since this farmland produced a lot of deer, it was inevitable that hunting would be required to cull the herd. Grandson Braylon got his first deer on this piece of property. It was an off-hand shot after just jumping off the ATV. Nice shot! Grandson Mason also shot his first buck on the property, and it was from a range of 345 yards. That's some pretty accurate shooting! The boys are being taught at an early age how to respect and safely handle firearms. Every young kid should learn this lesson. While there on one of our visits, we practiced shooting up on the mountain. A right of way for a major gas line runs through the property and, as such, free gas is provided to the property owner for life. What a deal. A one-foot diameter metal target was set up along the gas line clearing 365 yards away. I got to shoot Brett's sniper rifle at that distance and hit the target five times in a row. It was easy to shoot with the expertly set up rifle and scope. Brett has actually shot a 9-point buck at a distance of 220 yards with that rifle. Not as long a shot as his son, but still a respectable distance. On a darker note, the farmhouse was broken into during the first year of ownership. All the copper wiring and plumbing were ripped out of the house. Tools were stolen. Police were notified and are still investigating. I don't think anyone has ever been caught. Following this incident, our son installed a security system consisting of lights, alarms, and video. He can monitor the house remotely from Connecticut. He can even talk to the deer munching on garden plants near the front porch. Great technology.

West Virginia. Beautiful country, beautiful people. I can't wait to go back and make more memories there.

DOCTORS

I was fired by my doctor. We had gone to a specific primary care physician (PCP) in Connecticut for years. He was the doctor who attended to my broken ribs from a fall on black ice (not being racist) and examined me for my annual physical. We really liked this family doctor and trusted his medical decisions. When we bought a winter getaway house in The Villages, Florida, we planned to be there for just a few months in the winter to escape the cold. According to plan, we stayed for three months the first year, then four or five months the following year, and finally six months the next year. Once we passed the six-month mark, we became residents of Florida, saving us $7,000 or more in Connecticut state income tax each year. Since we were spending more time in Florida, we needed to find a PCP who could attend to us here if we needed medical attention. We were "snowbirds" during these transition years, and eventually, we sold our Connecticut home and became full-time residents of Florida. In the meantime, we preferred to keep our northern doctor in case we needed medical attention while visiting our kids and grandkids. At some point in these transition years, I received a package from Connecticut with all my medical records. Our old PCP said that he could no longer be responsible for my health since we were spending most, if not all, of our time down south. The realization set in that I had, out of necessity, been fired by my doctor. In fact, now we needed to find a dentist and other specialty care professionals to replace the ones we left up north. It took years to find the best doctors and dentists in Connecticut, and now we were starting all over again.

We leaned on our new friends in The Villages for recommendations for doctors and specialists. It seems like there is a big turnover in PCPs in Florida. We are currently on our fourth PCP in eleven years. Maybe doctors in the retirement state of Florida get burnt out from caring for old people, or maybe they don't make as much money from Medicare patients as they would from young people. We have found that it sometimes takes weeks or months to see a professional for things like Urology, ENT, elective surgery, or dermatology. Of course, emergency services are available right away at local hospitals or satellite emergency rooms. Fire and medical emergency services are quite good in The Villages. It's not unheard of that a 911 call will be answered in less than five minutes which is a pretty good response time. We also have automated emergency defibrillators (AEDs) located in a number of places in our neighborhood. Brenda and I are both trained in the usage of this equipment. We've had several alerts that we have responded to, but luckily, we have never had to apply chest compression or use the AED thus far. One of our neighbors who trained with us actually saved the life of a man during a church service. You never know when the training will come in handy. The training we received no longer includes mouth-to-mouth breathing, but I jokingly tell friends that if they go down and need mouth-to-mouth, they are going to die! We have monthly alerts programmed to our cell phones with a special ringtone. We used to get the alerts on our landline phone, but after having a landline all our lives, we finally "cut the cord" and went digital. Old habits die hard. I still glance at the location in our house where the answering system and phone once stood to see if we have any messages. You gotta love the improvements in technology. We feel naked and out of touch without our cell phones near us.

Now that we have established all our specialty care people here in Florida, our calendar is full of appointments. We've come to accept that's the way it is when you get old. It takes more maintenance to keep the machine moving. None of us are going to escape this world without some kind of terminal medical emergency. We've lost good friends from heart attacks, brain tumors, Lou Gehrig's disease (ALS), Alzheimer's, Parkinson's disease, stroke, and even mosquito-borne West Nile virus. Damn! I'm getting bummed out! I think I'll have a double Jack Daniels on the rocks tonight before bedtime.

DENTISTS

I have gone to medical and dental doctors all my life, just like everyone else has had to do for maintenance and emergency visits. It's a fact of life. You cannot avoid it. As a kid, I visited our local dentist from time to time to have cavities filled and for general cleanings. As the years went on, I probably didn't take as good care of my teeth as I should have. There were too many distractions like school and work. When I met my wife, Brenda, I started going to their family dentist in Hartford, Connecticut. This doctor/dentist was old school, and while pretty good, he apparently did not keep up with all the latest methods and procedures. It wasn't long before we were referred to a dentist in Wethersfield, Connecticut. We went to him for a number of years. Brenda worked in his office for a while when she was re-entering the workforce. My suspicions grew about this new dentist when he attempted to do a root canal on me, a procedure usually done by a specialist. After 10 or 12 shots of Novocaine, I was still jumping out of the chair in pain as he probed through the tooth and into the canal. He either used cheap

Novocaine or didn't know the exact place to inject it. This turned out to be one of the worst experiences I ever had in a dental chair. Something like this will put the fear of God in you and make you think twice about ever going back to a dentist. Somebody in a Doctor of Dental Medicine or Doctor of Dental Surgery program has to graduate at the bottom of their class. I think we just found the guy who did. I'm surprised he actually graduated at all.

Dental hygienists are like nurses. They know the good doctors and the ones they would not send their mother to. Eventually, at the suggestion of our dental hygienist up north, we gravitated to a family practice in Glastonbury, Connecticut. I've always wondered why they call dental and medical businesses a "practice." Are these so-called 'professionals' just practicing on us? I'd like to think not, but I am still suspicious about this term. Our new dentist, Dr. Steve Balloch, was really good. A true professional. He went to school while in the military and turned out to be a real artist in his chosen field. He performed difficult dental procedures on us, like implants, crowns, and overlays. My two front teeth were stained from a fever I had as a kid, and the overlays covered those imperfections. Crowns and implants replaced removable bridges that our old dentist in Hartford had performed years ago. That was old-school stuff. We were also referred to a periodontist, Dr. Ernie Spira, for gum-related procedures and an endodontist for painless root canal work. Our perio guy was funny. I loved his sense of humor. He would make me laugh until tears flowed out of my eyes, all while performing radical surgery on my gums. He was so good, and maybe even a little vain, that the license plate on his personal car read "TOP GUM." We went to these professionals for years until we became full-time residents in Florida.

Now we had to find good, qualified dentists here, which took years for us to find in Connecticut. TOP GUM actually recommended a few colleagues in Florida who were top-notch. We also found good people by referral from neighbors and friends.

We have been fortunate to find good dental hygienists to take care of us. Usually, they were young women and they did fantastic work. Training for them is akin to studying to be a registered nurse. Our former Glastonbury hygienist was unavailable for one appointment, so a new DMD in the office was substituted to perform my cleaning. I could tell right away that he was not doing a thorough job. I considered myself an expert in having my teeth cleaned by the best hygienists, and I could feel his methods were not very good. After the cleaning and at a subsequent visit, I let Dr. Balloch know that his new DMD was not that great. Other patients must have made similar comments because the new guy didn't last long. Maybe he joined the practice with the Wethersfield dentist who graduated at the bottom of his class! My new hygienist, Tori, in Florida, is a super girl. She is so nice that I get a big hug from her every time she finishes my cleaning. She has earned my respect and I let her know she is appreciated. We are lucky to have found top-notch professional dental folks in Florida. I suspect these people may have graduated near the top of their class! Just saying.

TREES

One of my first encounters with trees was when I was a young boy growing up in central Massachusetts. A bunch of us kids were climbing a big one near our house and just generally hanging out. I had climbed up to about fifteen feet above the ground and shimmied out onto a branch. Somehow, I lost my grip and plummeted to the ground, landing on my back. What do they say... It's not the fall; it's the sudden stop at the bottom that hurts! There was no real pain from the fall because I landed on thick grass, but I couldn't move and just lay there trying to regain my breath. What a weird, serene sensation that was. After a minute or two (seemed like it was much longer), I finally was able to start breathing again. Now I knew, quite literally, what it felt like to get the "wind knocked out of me." It was not a good feeling and I wouldn't recommend it to anybody. I believe it was the only time in my life I experienced something like that. Thank God for small blessings.

The piece of land that our house was situated on in Clinton, Massachusetts was about ¾ of an acre in size. At the far corner of our property, at the intersection of Chace and Water Streets, stood an old sugar maple tree. This was the kind of tree that could be tapped in the springtime to capture sap flowing up to the branches. The sap would then be boiled to reduce it to maple syrup, a real treat in New England. This majestic tree was beautiful, especially in the fall when its leaves turned a golden color. It was more than three feet in caliper and it must have been well over 100 years old. At some point in time, the towns of Clinton and Bolton decided to dig up the adjacent roads to install water or sewer lines. When they did this, it exposed the roots of the tree for a long period of time. I'm told that the root system of a tree extends out to the drip line of the branches, so many of the roots of this tree had been severed. It wasn't long after that the tree showed signs of distress and eventually died. Because the town had caused the damage, they were tasked with cutting the tree down at their cost. What a tragic loss of a beautiful specimen of a sugar maple tree. Life goes on.

In front of our house stood a mature Ash tree. It was located near a well that was on the farm property when my folks purchased the land. I remember this tree vividly as a child because I had to rake the huge amount of leaves that fell from it every fall. One of my favorite uncles, Wally Ackerman from Long Island, spent time with us kids under this tree playing mumbly-peg. It was a game using a jack knife to perform various tricks which are a little hard to describe. Let's just say that each trick required the blade to successfully stick in the ground. It was a harmless version of the game which apparently was concocted by soldiers during WWI and WWII to pass the time. During the 4th of July weekend when many of our neighbors were traveling or were at their summer cottages, my dad trimmed the Ash tree… with his 12-gauge shotgun! The neighbors that were still there didn't mind too much because they were making noise by shooting off fireworks. Loaded up with buckshot, Dad took aim at dead branches in the tree and fired away. He was actually quite successful using this pruning method. One time he turned his attention to a couple of blue spruce trees we had in the yard and trimmed about two feet off the tops of them also! It was just Dad being 'dear old Dad.' My mother put up with his impulsiveness.

When we retired to Florida, we had to learn about a new species of trees. Palms. Research revealed that there are over 2,500 varieties of palms in the south of the United States. We traded the sound of rustling leaves in the wind for the much different sound of palm fronds swaying in the breeze. Definitely a different sound. Of course, the movement of air is much warmer here so that adds to the sweetness of the sound. Some palm trees are in the date family, and so they annually drop their messy seeds that look similar to date nuts. It is kind of like the acorns that oak trees drop up north. We don't have red oak or white oak trees here in Florida; we have live oaks that actually look like they are dead with Spanish moss hanging from their branches. Apparently, Spanish moss is a member of the pineapple family, although you couldn't prove it to me. When my parents took a trip to Florida years ago, my dad remarked that Spanish moss reminded him of dirty dish rags hanging off the branches. I actually have to agree with his assessment. Live oak trees were planted around southern homes for shade and protection from hurricanes. You can actually feel the drop in perceived temperature when you go from the hot sun to the shade of a live oak tree. That was considered air conditioning in "old Florida." It is springtime as I write this story, and the story wouldn't be complete without mentioning pollen which starts extra early and ends extra late in Florida. The greenish, brownish remnants can be washed from our lanai, sidewalks, and driveway on a daily basis. We have developed some new allergic reactions to this type of pollen, but fortunately, it is not life-threatening. We just suck it up and live with it as Floridians. It is the time of year when everything begins to come alive after a brief winter. Crepe myrtle trees get pruned back so far that they call it crepe murder. They look like stumps but amazingly spring back to life with the hint of warmer weather. Before long, they are in full bloom and have blossoms of white, pink, and red. The sweet smell of jasmine is also in the air. These fragrant bushes are everywhere and the smell is unmistakably satisfying. Living here in Florida is much different than where we came from in New England, that's for sure. And we are learning to love it!

I couldn't talk about trees without mentioning a little ditty that my dad used to say. It goes like this. "Through the treeses blow the breezes; if I don't get a ride, I'll walk by Jesus!" It's really funny the silly stuff you heard as a kid and still remember all these years later. Good memories.

WILDLIFE

I lived in Connecticut for most of my adult life. We were fortunate to own a new house as newlyweds in the town of Coventry. As our family grew, we moved to another new house in Manchester. It was closer to work and our children's activities. As our kids eventually grew up and married, we built another house not far away in a new development. Since we were the first to build in this neighborhood, we got the pick of the lots. We selected a lot at the top of the hill overlooking downtown Hartford and the Connecticut River Valley seven miles away. The Metacomet Ridge on the horizon was seventeen miles away. The lot was located on a cul-de-sac and the rear of the house backed up to an old Nike missile base and many acres of woodland. During one of the first nights sleeping at the new house, we were awakened by a blood-curdling animal sound in the woods behind us. The next morning, I investigated the area thinking I would find blood and guts everywhere, but I never did find any evidence or remains of the previous night's altercation. In the coming days we were witness to all kinds of animal activity. Not too long ago, this was the territory of wild animals and we had infiltrated their domain. We spotted deer on a regular basis. During the mating season, it was not unusual to see a big buck strutting his stuff as he searched for a doe to mate with. One day I came home from work and found the turf in our back yard all torn up! There must have been one helluva orgy going on while our backs were turned!

Over the ten years that we lived at this location, we were privy to seeing all kinds of wildlife, like the red fox that hunted this area for a while. We saw him carrying a gray squirrel that he had caught, and many times, he would catch a chipmunk for a snack. How the hell he ever caught one of those little critters always amazed me. Those little suckers are fast! I guess it's a survival thing. If you're hungry, you'll find a way to 'git 'er done. We had a family of skunks come through the yard one day. The little babies had a hard time climbing over the stone wall at the back of our property. It was cute to watch, but the grandkids who were visiting at the time wanted to help the little ones over the wall. We quickly poo-pooed that idea! We also saw wild turkeys from time to time. They had been reintroduced into Connecticut in the 1970s after being absent for a hundred years or more. They were big birds that sometimes got a little aggressive. The grandkids were frightened of them. We had a neighbor who had a habit of throwing out seeds and bread-crumbs to feed the animals. Crows quickly figured out where the free stuff was and flocked to the area. They became such a nuisance that I eliminated a few of them with my air rifle. Squirrels, too. It was a sporting thing. Some people won't agree, but it doesn't matter how many of them you eliminate. They just keep reproducing.

When we finally retired to Florida and sold the Connecticut house, we had to learn about all the new kinds of animals we would be confronted with. We had squirrels here, too. So many, that we had to relocate them to a better neighborhood, so to speak. They would climb on our pool lanai screens and pee on the decking below. I could not shoot them because of the proximity to other homes, so I relented and bought a HAVAHART trap. It wasn't long before I trapped and relocated as many as 30 squirrels! I've even caught two at once, an adult and a little one. I left the trap out overnight once. When I checked the trap the next morning, it was filled with a huge opossum! Geez, that thing was really big, smelled bad, and bared its teeth as I grabbed the trap. I couldn't wait to get rid of him. I went on to catch more of these critters, but none as big as that first one.

A neighbor lady had her little dog snatched by a coyote. She let him out unattended at night in the backyard to do his thing. The coyote did his thing. He must have been hungry. There are also big hawks and eagles that can swoop down and grab these little pets for a meal. I saw a video recently where an eagle actually picked up a young child. His mother rescued him, but it just goes to show how big and powerful these predators can be. You do not want to leave your little buddy unattended in the yard in Florida, that's for sure. We've heard stories of people walking their dogs next to a pond. Every pond or body of water in Florida has an alligator. One lady recently was protecting her dog from an alligator attack, and she ended up getting dragged into the water and dying. It's a different world down here in the Deep South. I was in the hot tub early one morning and I spotted a bobcat walking on the villa wall behind our house. This was their territory not too long ago and you don't have to look too far to see them still stalking the neighborhood. Did I mention snakes? We are vigilant everywhere we go, so we avoid poisonous ones like rattlesnakes and cottonmouths, also known as water moccasins. The latter variety can be aggressive and has been known to climb right into a fisherman's boat. A friend of ours was golfing and went to retrieve his ball near a pond. A black snake that was lying there struck at him and caught the fabric of his pants near the zipper. It was a cottonmouth. This attack could have turned out to be a lot worse. Fortunately, we have only seen non-poisonous garden snakes around our house. The black racer is the most prevalent. You've got to have situational awareness at all times in Florida. It's definitely not the same as living in New England.

Tragically, we had a good friend who was bitten by a mosquito while sitting around a recreation center fire pit after golfing with the guys. He started acting strangely a couple of days later, so was taken to the local hospital. After a week of testing and indecision, his health deteriorated, and he was transferred to a hospital in Gainesville where he was diagnosed with West Nile virus. Other complications set in, and he eventually died from this disease. Very sad. It is a different life here in Florida. Most of us will survive, some will not.

We spotted this alligator in the front yard of a neighbor's house and couldn't resist taking a picture of it. We think this is pretty humorous because alligators are everywhere there is a body of water in Florida. This one was a true Floridian sporting sunglasses! OK, it's not alive, but it sure looked like it!

SINKHOLES

Sinkholes occur all over the world. Every state in the United States has them except for possibly Rhode Island and Delaware. We certainly have our fair share of sinkholes in Florida. Other states that are known to have an abundance of sinkholes are Texas, Pennsylvania, Alabama, Missouri, Kentucky, and Tennessee. The biggest sinkhole on record is in China. It measures over two thousand feet deep and is known as the "heavenly pit." The biggest sinkhole in the United States is in Alabama. It is about 120 deep and is called the "Golly Hole." Ironically, the sinkhole capital of the US is Fountain, Minnesota. It has more sinkholes than people! Many sinkholes occur naturally, but some of them are caused by human activity. One example, while not a sinkhole, was something I witnessed while going to school in California. My aunt and uncle lived in Palos Verdes Estates on a hillside overlooking Catalina Island. Construction near the top of the hill triggered a landslide and the entire community of Portuguese Bend started sliding slowly into the sea. The rate of movement was only a few inches per month, but over a long period of time, large crevices opened up. Houses near the ocean were either destroyed or moved to another location by barge. Route 1 along the coast had to be constantly repaired due to the "jog" in the road. Utilities had to be located above ground. This area is still sliding into the sea from when it first started more than 50 years ago.

Over the last fourteen years we have lived in Florida, we have witnessed many instances of sinkholes. Much of Florida sits on a porous limestone base that contains the aquifer from which we get our potable water. When it rains, some of the limestone is washed away. During dry spells, the water table is lowered, opening up large caverns. Sometimes the land above the caverns collapses and creates a sinkhole. And let me tell you, when it rains in Florida, it really rains. It can be raining on one side of the street and not on the other. When clouds open up, they dump whatever moisture they have been storing, which is usually a deluge. When we first drove to Florida years ago, we had to follow the taillights of a tractor-trailer for the final miles of our trip. It was nighttime and it was raining buckets of water. Welcome to the Sunshine State!

We have a couple of golf driving ranges in The Villages where you hit your ball into a lake. The balls are designed to float and are scooped up by a retrieval crew during the night. There are floating islands in the lake which can be used as targets. I have been trying unsuccessfully to land a ball on those damn islands for years. I haven't given up yet! On at least one occasion I know of, a sinkhole opened up under one of the lakes and swallowed all the water and golf balls. The problem was mitigated by dumping clay soil into the cavern, thereby plugging the leak. In time, water found its way back into the depression, and before too long, it was a lake again. Only in Florida. In the last 40 years, just two incidents of people dying from a sinkhole have been reported. The most recent of which was in 2013 in the Tampa area. A house fell into a sinkhole during the night. There were five occupants in the house at the time. Four escaped; one did not. One man tried to rescue his brother but was unsuccessful. The man's body was never recovered.

In our neighborhood, we have had a few instances of sinkholes occurring. The most remarkable of which was our friends Ken and Donna who own a house near us. Ken was outside doing yard work. All of a sudden, the ground beneath him collapsed, and he found himself almost up to his hip in a hole. Experts were contacted to use ground penetrating radar to evaluate the extent of the situation. A deep sinkhole was detected directly beneath his house. Over the coming weeks, over sixty cement trucks entered our neighborhood, each carrying ten cubic yards of cement slurry. The slurry was pumped into pipes that were located all around and inside the house. Ken now has the deepest foundation of any house in the neighborhood! The ironic part of the story is that Ken and his wife lived in the house while the work was being done. If that were me, I would not have been able to sleep a wink. Just saying. Ken's great insurance company (Chubb) paid for all the repair work, which probably approached the $100,000 mark.

Because of sinkhole problems in Florida over the years, insurance companies worked with the state government to change the law in their favor. Most insurance companies only provide "catastrophic" sinkhole coverage now, which means your house has to pretty much fall into the hole to be covered, and out-of-pocket expenses are high. After our neighbor's experience, we changed our insurance to Chubb (not an endorsement), which provides full sinkhole coverage. If we have partial damage due to a sinkhole, we are covered. It's expensive insurance, but we look at it as the cost of doing business in Florida. We are protecting one of our largest investments.

It is reported that over 5,000 people a week are relocating to Florida. It's a wonderful place to live in spite of sinkholes. No state income tax saves residents lots of money. Florida is aptly named the "Sunshine State" where 'you don't have to shovel sunshine'! Come on down!

TEACHING

I have never been formally trained to be a teacher. We have a daughter who has a master's degree in education. As she went through the student-teacher program, I never understood why schools don't have to pay at least minimum wage for the many hours of mandatory classroom teaching. It's the same for nursing programs which require a number of hours of clinical, hands-on training with no pay. If you want to encourage qualified people to be interested in these disciplines, they should get paid.

Parents are essentially teachers. Teaching children the difference between right and wrong starts at an early age. I'm sure there are books about how to bring up children, but I have never read one. Maybe I should have but I think people read those kinds of books when they realize they need help in raising their kids. My wife, Brenda, and I just used common sense. It doesn't mean that we were always right, but I think we did a pretty good job. Brenda also brought our daughter and son to church to teach them to become good Christians. Do unto others as you would have them do unto you. The golden rule. Our children were taught in the public elementary school system until the 5th grade but continued in Catholic schools for the 6th through 12th grades. Junior and senior public high schools in our town were not rated very highly. We wanted to give our children the best primary education available, so we opted for private schools. It was expensive and we never understood why we still had to pay taxes for the public school system when our kids were not sitting in a public-school classroom. Some compensation or reduction in taxes should have been provided. I really admire parents who homeschool their children. I can imagine it takes a lot of effort and planning to do that. I've read that these children do much better than their public school counterparts when they go on to higher education.

With no formal training, I began teaching concealed carry pistol permit classes at our local shooting club. I competed in pistol matches and did quite well. It was a subject that I loved, so talking about shooting safely came easy to me. Hell, I had been handling guns since I was a kid. My dad was a good teacher. I began teaching a segment of the class with two other instructors. We all had been trained in a course given by the National Rifle Association (NRA) and we were all certified instructors. I loved the feeling when I knew I had the class's attention. When I introduced humor into a lesson, it was fun to watch the students' reactions. It was very gratifying knowing that your teaching skills were being appreciated. As it turns out, I am still teaching pistol permit classes to friends and neighbors in our retirement community. I've been doing this for thirty years and have taught over 1,000 students.

One of the presentations I had to make when I worked at Pratt & Whitney Aircraft Engines was daunting. I was always uneasy speaking in front of a crowd, large or small. It was definitely not my forte in life. I was selected to speak at an airline conference in Los Angeles. This is something that our company did annually for representatives of the airlines who flew our engines. Typically, there would be 700 or 800 attendees at the conference, and I was selected to be one of the speakers on the stage. Apprehensive doesn't come close to describing the initial fear I had in preparing for this presentation. My subject was Low Pressure Turbine modules that were having some mechanical difficulties in the field. Our experimental department was working on fixes to be incorporated when the engines came off the wing for overhaul. I worked for weeks with professional trainers to fine-tune my speaking skills and refine my technical presentation. Did you know that if you are using a laser pen to point to something on a large screen, your hand will shake from being nervous, and that is amplified on the screen? The easy fix is to just steady your hand on the podium. I didn't know that, but I quickly learned and adopted this technique. The bottom line is that I successfully gave my presentation without a hitch and was congratulated by the VP of Engineering. This experience gave me the confidence to speak in front of individuals and groups of people, large or small.

Pickleball is our main sport in retirement. I was trained as a pickleball instructor in The Villages and taught there for seven years. We brought the game to a variety of towns in Connecticut. There was no place to play in and around our hometown of Manchester, so Brenda and I joined the USA Pickleball Association and became ambassadors for the sport. Of course, it was self-serving because we would be creating places to play when we were up north in the summer months. We taught people how to safely play the game in several towns, and now, years later, there are hundreds of people playing the sport with many indoor and outdoor courts being provided for the general public. Teaching this sport to others is very gratifying and we have met so many nice people because of our efforts. Giving that large presentation years ago in Los Angeles gave me the confidence, skills, and knowledge to have fun teaching others to play pickleball, shoot a gun safely, and interact with people in a friendly, relaxed atmosphere. It's funny how things play out in life. I guess I am a teacher after all even though I have never been formally trained. Similarly, my dad used to say, "I'm a poet and don't know it!" Our children turned out just fine. Life is good.

EDUCATION

Education, of course, is important. There is no guarantee, but a good education gives you the advantage of going on in life and possibly earning a good living. I had always been good at math and found early learning pretty easy. Some people struggle for whatever reason. I graduated from a two-year technical program in aircraft maintenance and went on to get a Bachelor of Science degree in engineering. I earned good money working in the Experimental Test department at Pratt & Whitney Aircraft and retired after 43 years. A good pension was a bonus. I met my wife, Brenda, at Pratt. She really wanted to go into nursing, but her family could not afford it so she financed her own education at Hartford Secretarial School and entered that field of work. While at Pratt, she went to community college and obtained an associate degree in general studies. The company paid for everything and awarded her an additional $5,000 in stock as an incentive. After a period of time, she went back to school and obtained her Bachelor of Arts degree. Again, this was paid for by the company with a $5,000 stock award. She was on a roll now and took an online course for her Master's degree in Psychology. The company awarded her another $5,000 in stock. She aced all her courses, so she will forever be known as 'my little smart-ass wife!'

Our kids, Kimberly and Brett, both started their higher education by obtaining associate degrees at the local community college. They went on to get BS and Master's degrees. I guess they take after Brenda. I contemplated going for a Master's degree but decided that I neither wanted it nor needed it to earn a good living. I'm content with my level of learning.

My parents never went to high school. They both went as far as the eighth grade and then entered the job market to help support the family. They worked in local factories all their lives and earned a decent living with hard work and determination. They even helped finance my education, for which I will be eternally grateful. Brenda's parents went a little further in school. Joe went as far as his second year in high school but had trouble with mathematics. He quit school and a year or two later, joined the Army, lying about his age to get in. Brenda's mom, Bridget, completed high school. Again, with hard work and determination, she and Joe earned a good enough living to survive and raise a family.

I am a firm believer that you do not need a higher education to have a good life. Some people are just not cut out for it. Some people obtain a degree but then do nothing with it. The education is not wasted but could have been put to better use. I know people who were brilliant in school but could not get along with coworkers or team with others. I also know people who received good educations but never really loved the field they were working in for the entirety of their lives. I was lucky. My education had everything to do with aviation, and I knew from an early age that I would have something to do with airplanes. There were some hiccups along the way, but basically, I loved the field that I was in.

Some folks go to technical schools to learn a trade because they are hands-on kind of people. I think that is a smart move. Many parents push their kids to get a college education, thinking it is necessary to earn a good living. But there is a lot of money to be made in, for example, the construction, plumbing, electrical, and automotive trades. Also, nursing, dental hygienist, electronics technician, landscape designer, web developer, and heavy equipment operator are all good-paying jobs. The possibilities are endless. Another avenue is to join one of the military branches, complete your obligation, and go to college or technical school upon discharge... all paid for by the government. I've known folks who started working in a trade and then went on to start their own businesses and have done quite well. Good for them. Of course, there are people who have never done a day of hard work in their lives. Some government programs available these days actually promote this type of behavior. This is wrong in so many ways. That old 19th century saying, 'Give a man a fish and you feed him for a day. Teach a man to fish, and you feed him for a lifetime,' is still appropriate in this day and age.

My dad lectured me years ago to "use your head instead of your back." Smart guy, and he only had an eighth-grade education. He went to the school of hard knocks. I remember him telling anyone who would listen that he went through Harvard. Dad wasn't talking about the prestigious university. He was talking about the nearby town of Harvard, Massachusetts! No lie. Fact. He had driven through the town many times. Another quip that comes to mind is that engineers, while technically smart, are notoriously bad with their command of the English language. So, the saying goes, "I always wanted to be an engineer, and now I are one!" Funny stuff.

RELIGION

My parents were members of the German Congregational Church in Clinton, Massachusetts which was formed in 1887. My maternal and paternal grandparents all came directly from Germany through Ellis Island in the late 1800s, so they naturally gravitated to this church. The church was located in a part of town where people from the old country tended to congregate. That part of town was known, of course, as 'German town.' Clustered in other neighborhoods of Clinton were Polish, Irish, and Italian folks. I suspect that people from the same ethnic backgrounds tend to live near each other in their adopted country for comfort, safety, and social reasons. Our church held a service in German proceeded by another service in English. This was done to satisfy the elderly folks who wanted to carry on in the tradition of the old country. The younger generation, who were born in the United States, preferred services in English. As time went on, the old folks died off, and the German service was eliminated. Only the occasional hymn was sung in German to remind us of our heritage. Many years later, our church was combined with another ecumenical Christian church and renamed the United Church of Christ (UCC). In 1961, a Methodist church in town closed its doors and joined with the UCC. During my childhood, Mother was active in the Ladies' Aid Society and my dad served as superintendent of the Sunday school for a time. In my early teens, I was selected to go to a Christian camp in New Hampshire for a week. It was a fun week because we did all kinds of activities, including swimming, hiking Mount Monadnock, shooting archery, and firing 22-caliber rifles on the range. On Sunday we all attended the huge church on campus. It reminded me of a tabernacle. The three-hour service was a bit long for a kid. I would have been okay with just one hour. One and done!

As I grew up and went away to college, I didn't attend church that often. I still identified as a Christian but I didn't glean much from most church services and sermons. After college, I went to work for Pratt & Whitney Aircraft in East Hartford, Connecticut. That is where I met my future wife, Brenda. Since she was Roman Catholic and I was Protestant, I had to meet with a priest prior to getting married and consent to having our children raised in the Catholic faith. I had no problem with that since it was a Christian faith and we all answer to the same higher authority. My mom, on the other hand, was devastated that I was going to marry a French Catholic girl. She always wanted me to marry a Protestant German girl. Let's just say it took my mom a while to get over the shock. Our wedding was held in St. Augustine Church in Hartford. The ceremony was somewhat ecumenical since our minister from Clinton also took part in the service. We had to appease mom and dad. As of this writing, Brenda and I just celebrated our 55th wedding anniversary in the spring. I found a good girl. My parents would be proud.

Now retired in Florida, one of the first things you notice down south is the number of churches. You see them everywhere you go. A lot of them are situated on a county road, often referred to as church row. Our Daily Sun newspaper lists all of the area church services in the Saturday edition. I was just looking at that section of the paper and was amazed to count 29 denominations and 159 churches! The ones that I am most familiar with are Baptist, Roman Catholic, Jehovah's Witnesses, Lutheran, Judaism, Methodist, Presbyterian, and, of course, United Church of Christ. There are no German Congregational churches here for some reason. Go figure. You don't hear too much about other denominations like Baha'i, Metropolitan, Pentecostal, Seventh-Day Adventist, Messianic Judaism, and the like, but they are here. In our travels in nearby rural Summerfield, we stumbled across a cowboy church complete with hitching posts and water troughs! In Oxford, there is a farm called Barb's Barn. It is an old Florida cowboy kind of place where they have weekly country music gatherings. But on Sunday, they have a country church service in the barn that people can attend. I think that's kinda cool. I guess it doesn't matter where you get your religion from as long as you connect in some way with the big guy upstairs, act like a Christian in all things you do, and 'shine your light.'

BOOKS

I went to a Book Expo here in The Villages, Florida in January of 2020. I had heard about the Expo at a New Year's Eve party from a lady by the name of Rita Boehm. She was a published author and, at the time, president of the Writer's League of The Villages (WLOV). This was also just about the time COVID-19 was kicking into high gear. I had been thinking about writing a book and the Expo was the perfect venue to attend to learn how to do it. There were probably 100 authors selling their books at this event and the public turnout was amazing. A couple of seminars were being offered. I attended the one concentrating on how to publish your new book. John Prince was the main speaker and I found him very interesting and informative. He talked about his publishing company in The Villages and how they worked with Amazon to get independent authors into print. I met with John after his presentation and got his business card. I came home with lots of ideas swimming through my head.

Research that I had done about writing a book informed me that lots of people make the attempt to write a book, but most don't get too far and quit. I was determined to succeed and with the Covid pandemic in full swing, there would be a lot of downtime to write. There are all kinds of genres and subjects to write about. You've got mystery, horror, fantasy, romance, science fiction, history, biography, adventure, children, young adult, memoir... the list goes on and on. I figured out pretty quickly that I did not have the capacity or imagination to write, let's say, a mystery novel. What I did have, however, was a good memory of events that had happened during my lifetime that might be interesting to readers. I can't remember what I had for breakfast or what I did yesterday, but I can remember in great detail things that happened in my childhood. Funny how the brain works. I must have a big file cabinet somewhere in the coconut sitting on my shoulders! My book would be a memoir.

And so it began. I dedicated the quiet morning hours to writing my thoughts and experiences on the computer. My wife, Brenda, was the first to edit my ramblings. She suggested corrections and pointed out typographical errors, which I appreciated. I was in constant contact with John who I selected as my publisher. About this time, he entered into a collaboration with other authors to create Hallard Press. These folks would be instrumental in getting my first book published. I struggled with naming my new book. After a number of iterations, I decided to call it *I'm Almost History*. This title would be apropos because, well, I'm old and I'm about to become a part of history. I thought at first that I would just write this book for my family. I wrote about things that I had never told them or they never knew about me. Our son and daughter might find it interesting. Maybe not. My grandkids might be interested.

Maybe, even someday, my great-grandchildren could read about their great-grandpa. In the end, I had the book published for all the world to see.

When the writing was completed, it was time for editing. John took my thumb drive with all the information on it and forwarded the manuscript to his sister in Canada. A few weeks later, I got the edited copy back for my perusal. An editor looks for grammar, punctuation, and spelling (GPS). I always thought I had a pretty good command of the English language but, apparently not! I couldn't believe the changes. Not to the content of the story but to GPS. Next, I submitted the pictures that would be included in most chapters. John then went to work paginating and formatting my manuscript. A preface and index of chapters also had to be developed. John helped me design the front and back covers for the book. I would be remiss if I did not mention Chris and Pat Beltrami who critiqued and photo-shopped many of the pictures included in and on the book. Talented people. Oh, and I can't forget the Library of Congress and ISBN numbers, which are important and unique identifiers for records and libraries. This was all part of the publishing process.

It wasn't long before I got my first proof book from Amazon. What a great feeling of accomplishment to finally have a finished book of my own writing in my hands. I joined the WLOV at the suggestion of John at Hallard Press. I got a lot of free advertising through this organization and Hallard to promote sales. I never got into this book-writing thing to make a lot of money, and I didn't. But I still get royalties from Amazon books selling copies in the United States, England, Germany and Japan. I finally got a table at the 2023 Book Expo.

It was really fun selling signed copies of my own book. I also was featured at Barnes and Noble through the WLOV. Quite an honor, I must admit.

In 2022, I had another book published through John Prince and Hallard Press. It was *The Deuce Coupe That Stole My Heart*. This book was all about cars that I've had in my lifetime and the story about building my 1932 Ford coupe. My first book leaned heavily towards aviation and the second was all about cars. All this leads up to this, my third book. Regrettably, I will have to find a way to get it published without the help of my friend, John Prince. John was diagnosed with a brain tumor and recently passed away. He will be sorely missed, and I will forever remember his help and friendship in publishing my first two books. God rest his soul.

Politics

My parents were registered Republicans. They voted a split ticket. If a Democrat was on the ballot and he or she was the best candidate, then they would vote for that person. My wife's family members were registered Democrats. I'm not sure what their voting record was like, but they were decent people and I'd bet good money that they voted a split ticket also.

Brenda and I are both currently registered as Republicans. We were, for a time, registered as Independents. In Florida, the only way you can vote in a primary is if you are registered in either party, and you can only vote for that party's candidates. When Mitt Romney was running for president in 2012, we switched back to the Republican party so we could vote in the primary. Mitt came to The Villages and we witnessed his speech in the town square. As it turns out, it was a big mistake voting for him. We always felt that we wasted our votes. He morphed into a RINO... Republican in name only! Like my dad used to say, "I wouldn't trust a politician as far as I could throw a piano, and that ain't too far!" Dear old Dad was right.

In 2016, Donald Trump was our candidate of choice. He ran against Hillary Clinton who was the typical politician claiming that half of Trump's supporters belong in a "basket of deplorables." She was talking about us. If we had done what Hillary had done with her emails, destroying evidence, we would be in jail right now. We are definitely seeing a two-tiered justice system. In spite of this, Trump won that year, and we are convinced that it was with the help of God. He went on to accomplish wonderful things for this country in spite of being impeached for abuse of power. This was the Democrat way of going after an opponent. And then along came COVID-19 in the spring of 2020, just in time for the next election. My GFI (gut feeling index) tells me that this was a contrived pandemic involving China and the opposition party. In spite of this worldwide catastrophe, Trump held huge rallies attracting tens of thousands of people while Biden sat in the safety of his base-ment giving online chats. During personal appearances, Biden could only collect a few token supporters, but you couldn't tell because of the complicit mainstream media's camera positions and subsequent reporting. This was fake news as Trump so aptly stated many times.

Biden went on to win the 2020 election, or so it seems. There was so much speculation about ballot harvesting, late-night data dumps, mail-in ballots that could be manipulated, voter fraud, and even dead people voting from the grave. Trump garnered more votes than he did in the 2016 election, and he still lost to the mentally challenged guy in the basement. How can that be? My GFI kicked in again and told me 'something is wrong.' Call me a conspiracy theorist if you like, but I will never believe the outcome of this election. We wonder if our legitimate votes actually count anymore. It's a sad time for America.

So here we are in a time leading up to the 2024 election. Trump is back in the race. By all accounts, he is the populist candidate. So what does the opposition do? They bring all kinds of contrived lawsuits against him to try to take him off the campaign trail and bankrupt him. Nasty stuff. If you watch CNN, MSNBC, and other left-wing news networks, you'd think that this behavior was perfectly legitimate. It is the weaponizing of the justice system. We are living in corrupt, third-world country times. We could use some Divine Intervention again. God help us. Ecclesiastes 10.1. "The heart of the wise inclines to the right, but the heart of the fool to the left."

We think that Donald Trump is the only person who can save this country. In its current state, with wide open borders, the country will never be the same as the one we loved, fought for, and grew up in. We pray for the best outcome in the next election. Lord, hear our prayer. God bless America.

WOKE

Woke is an adjective derived from African American English meaning "alert to racial prejudice and discrimination." It now encompasses broader injustices such as sexism and LGBT (lesbian, gay, bisexual, transgender) rights. White privilege and reparations for slavery are also calls for justice from left-leaning socialists and democrats. I have never felt like I was racist. If I liked somebody, it didn't matter if they were black, white, or yellow. I judged them on their kindness and intellect. We have the highest respect for some of our gay/lesbian friends. We play sports with them. We have painting and decorating folks who think 'outside the box,' and we have Realtor people who are a pleasure to work with. But I'm starting to rethink this whole idea because of what is being shoved in our faces every day. If you watch TV, the ads are now 80% black even though the black population comprises only 12% of the country. Asian is 6%, Hispanic is 19% and White is 64%. So why is 12% of the population controlling what we are fed on TV? Socialists are pressing forward with this agenda. Think about it. There are black colleges, black social media, black TV programs, black magazines, black beauty pageants, etc. To me, that's racist. And they call white people racist? I don't know about you, but I think I am becoming a racist with all the division being forced on us.

There is a movement calling for reparations for black people because, somewhere in past generations, they were slaves. None of my family has ever owned slaves, so why should I pay reparations to someone just because they feel it is owed to them? And don't forget, black people owned slaves, too, and still do in many parts of the world. I don't know about you, but this socialist crap has turned everything upside down and I'm sick of it. LGBT comprises only about 6% of the population of the United States, but from the rhetoric and gay pride demonstrations, you'd think the number was much higher. People have been "coming out of the closet" for years. An example of this is when Joe, an engineer I worked with, decided to become Josephine after his mother and father passed away. He did not want to shock them with the news while they were still alive. He was a good guy and a smart engineer. He never acted feminine but apparently always wanted to be a girl. This transgender thing really freaks me out because it is being encouraged in school systems around the country for very young children. In the case of Joe, he waited until later in life so as not to disappoint his parents. He also was old enough to decide what he really always wanted to be, and he waited until he was mature enough to make the decision. I don't think young children should be given this choice until later in life. I have read about so many regrets and suicides from making gender changes at a young age. Let them be children first and then let them make up their own minds later in life.

When I was growing up in the mid-nineteen fifties, if you were mechanically inclined and worked on cars, you learned that in a brake system, there is a master cylinder and slave cylinders in each wheel. We never thought of this as being racist. It was just a way of denoting parts of a car. They are probably called primary and secondary cylinders now. Male and female parts have always signified the "inny" or "outy" shape of an item. I'm not sure how they might be referred to now and I'm almost afraid to ask! I've never thought of this as being sexist, but now I'm just not so sure. Similarly, homes have master bedrooms and master bathrooms which were usually the largest rooms in the house for the head of the family. Now, we are being trained to call them primary bedrooms and primary bathrooms. If it's all the same to you, I'll just go with the old terms by which I've always known them, and I won't feel sexist for doing so. Actors and actresses were male and female actors. Now, the woke community refers to them all as just actors. It's got to be gender-neutral to be acceptable. Apparently, you've got to be politically correct to get along in today's world. I'm glad I am retired and out of the working environment. I wouldn't survive. Our kids and grandkids will have to learn to adapt.

Speaking of politically correct, look at the people appointed by Joe Biden, the current POTUS. He has surrounded himself with a staff of LGBTQI+ (yes, they keep adding on to this list) appointees. Openly gay Pete Buttigieg is the secretary of transportation, Karine Jean-Pierre is the black, gay press secretary, and a real winner is the overweight transgender Dr. Rachel Levine, the assistant secretary for health. How about bald-headed LGBTQ Sam Brinton, the nuclear energy specialist who identifies as non-binary and dresses as a woman? You can't make this stuff up. Instead of hiring the brightest and the best, this administration is going all-inclusive. And don't get me started on Kamala Harris, the vice president. Her ethnicity is Asian, Indian, and Jamaican, but they say she is black because it fits the narrative. If you listen to her talk, she doesn't sound like the brightest and the best to me. Just saying. I'll make a prediction. As of this writing, the 2024 election is almost upon us. If Donald Trump does not win the White (racist?) House in this election, we have lost the country that we know and love. God help us and God Bless America.

Environment

Global warming. That's what all the talk is about these days. I'm not sure why there is so much concern about this, but I'd bet dollars to donuts that someone is positioning themselves to make money on the deal. Lots of money. I mean, come on, environmentalists are concerned about a few cows farting methane gas into the atmosphere? There are approximately 90 million cows in the United States at any one time. The 'go green' folks are proposing to reduce the bovine population significantly and transition gullible minions to eating veggie burgers. I don't know about you, but I'm not giving up on red meat and my weekly steak on the grill.

Thirty-five percent of the population in the United States is over the age of fifty. That's approximately 120 million 'old farts' roaming around the country. A lot of methane gas is being produced by these old codgers. I suppose next, the green folks will want to reduce the population of old people since they are probably causing more environmental damage than cows. They might propose changes to Medicare. The reduction in coverage and available medications could make the Q-tips die off sooner. I wouldn't put anything past the new breed of legislators and regulators now trying to run the country.

Electric vehicles (EVs) are nothing new. There were car manufacturers in the early 1900s producing them. They never became popular for good reason. Gas and eventually diesel-powered vehicles were the sensible choice, probably because of cost, convenience, and range. When we first retired to The Villages, we needed a golf cart. We bought a used electric one from a neighbor. Electric carts are definitely much quieter than gas carts, so for that reason, people like them. It was nice at first, but then we experienced a few incidents that changed our point of view. With the cart batteries fully charged, we took off for a little jaunt around town. We did a little sightseeing in the afternoon, followed by a trip to the town square for dinner and dancing. On our way home after dark, we started to lose power, so much so that we had to turn the headlights off to generate enough power to make it up the incline of a tunnel. We barely made it home that evening. Other events like this happened in the coming weeks, so we finally sold the electric cart and switched to a gas-powered one. As a point of interest, this new gas cart served us well. We bought it for $6,000, upgraded gears and wheels, changed oil regularly, and sold it for $5,900 ten years later. That cart owed us nothing.

Batteries do not like cold weather. We know this from trying to start a car in New England on a cold winter night. Batteries also do not like heat. Heat is probably a bigger problem for batteries than cold, and I've read articles stating that up to a 30% reduction in range can be expected during extreme temperature conditions. So, if EV-powered cars have an advertised range of 300 miles, you can expect a reduction to approximately 210 miles in extreme temperature conditions ... if you're lucky. The age of batteries will also reduce range. If you change the batteries in your golf cart, it could cost up to $1,000, especially if you change from lead-acid to lithium batteries. For a car, the cost to replace batteries could be anywhere between $5,000 and $20,000. Not particularly attractive to me. The infrastructure to support EVs is not keeping pace with the industry. I, personally, would be stressed out trying to find a place to charge my vehicle on a trip, not to mention the wait times for plugging into a charger and the time to charge. Thanks, but no thanks.

The environmental impact of producing batteries is never mentioned by the media. The rare elements used in batteries are dug out of the ground either by slave labor in foreign countries or by big, diesel-powered equipment. The charging stations, in some cases, are powered by diesel generators. What's wrong with this picture? Are the 'green' people taking all of this into consideration? I think not. It doesn't fit their narrative. A more sensible approach to this technology might be a hybrid car like Toyota Prius. Battery power with a small gas engine for backup seems a little more sensible to me. A friend let me drive his new Tesla Model X electric vehicle. I've got to admit, the acceleration was exhilarating. The next day, I drove my gas-powered 1932 Ford hot rod to a show. The contrast in technology was striking. I'm still not sold on EVs. Hybrid ... maybe.

So much more can be said about global warming and the environment. We will not solve all the problems at this time or in this short story. Experts even take different sides of the argument. And how about that young Swedish girl, Greta Thunberg, who became a climate activist at the tender age of fifteen? I don't know about you, but I wouldn't believe anything I hear from a young child like Greta. The world went crazy over her and accepted everything she said as true. As for me, I'll just go with my gut feeling index (GFI) and stick with gasoline-powered vehicles for now; thank you very much!

DEATH

None of us are going to live forever. It's just a fact of life. Some people depart this world prematurely by accident, because of health issues, or by unforeseen circumstances like the COVID-19 pandemic that we were all exposed to. Let's face it, life is a crap shoot. If we knew in advance what we would be facing, it would probably scare the shit out of us, please excuse the French. It is probably better that we do not know what the future holds. Instead, we should enjoy each day to the fullest and tell our family and good friends how much we love them every chance we get. We try to do that every time we end a conversation with our children and grandchildren because you really never know if that will be the last time to say those precious words to that person. It's a morbid thought, but it's so important when you think about it.

I have said many times that I have cried more for the loss of a family dog than I have for the loss of a relative or friend. That is probably an awful thing to say, but family pets love you unconditionally and are a part of your lives for such a short time. Of course, I cared for relatives who were an integral part of our lives and prayed for them when they departed this life. I wish I could have done things differently when my parents passed away. My father was the first to leave at the age of 84. He was in the local Clinton, Massachusetts, hospital for the last week of his life. I took time off work to be with him as much as possible. We did not know this would be his final week on earth. During one visit, I sat him up in his hospital bed and gave him a shave, which he hadn't had for about a week. I thought it would be a kind and refreshing thing to do to make him feel better. On another visit, I remember his doctor sticking a needle in his back to remove fluid from his lungs. His heart was giving out, and he could not breathe deeply enough to expel the fluids. He died a couple of days later from congestive heart failure. I was not with him at the time of his death, but looking back, I wish I had been. I was a few miles away at the family house, and I remember looking in the direction of the hospital. A dark cloud hung over the area as he passed. It was probably a sign from God that he was being taken to heaven. I will never know for sure. I spent a week or so with Mother at the time of his funeral and burial. When we got to the cemetery and stepped out of the funeral director's limousine, my mother tensed up while holding my arm. The cemetery staff had opened up the wrong grave site! We got back in the limo with the plan to return later in the day to say our final goodbyes to Father. My mother exclaimed out loud, "Those damn Irishmen can't get anything right!" referring to the staff workers at the cemetery. We came back later in the day and put Dad in his final resting place.

Mother lived on for a number of years in the family house that she and Father built with their own hands. At the age of

93, a medical issue finally put Mother in the hospital and then in a nursing home for a few weeks. During this time, she was again admitted to the hospital with what turned out to be a burst intestine. She was transported to a larger hospital in Worcester by helicopter. After an operation, she succumbed a week later. I cried for the loss of my mother in the same way I cried for my dad. I realize that after the loss of parents, you never really forget them, but life does go on. It's hard to put it into words, but I remember a poem that I read in the obituary section of our newspaper after the death of a local woman; it was so appropriate. Her family wrote this poem, which is repeated annually on the anniversary of her passing. It goes like this:

> *I thought of you with love today*
> *but that is nothing new.*
> *I thought of you yesterday,*
> *and the day before that, too.*
>
> *Your memory is my keepsake*
> *with which I'll never part.*
> *God has you in his keeping,*
> *I have you in my heart.*
>
> *It broke my heart to lose you,*
> *but you didn't go alone,*
> *for part of me went with you*
> *the day God took you home.*

My wife, Brenda, lost her dad, Joe, to cancer. He avoided the hospital at all costs because he believed that if he went there, he would never come home. That prophecy turned out to be true, as he passed within a week of being admitted. It wasn't long after that Brenda lost her sister, Karen, to stomach cancer. Karen loved life and was only in her 40s when she passed. We were left with her daughter and our niece, Nicole, to care for in the foreseeable future. It is devastating to lose a sister, and even more so to lose a child. Brenda's mom, Bridget, took the loss heavily. But, again, life goes on. Bridget survived heart bypass surgery years later and lived a number of years in an elderly apartment complex. We were with Bridget when she passed. This is the first time in my life that I was actually with a person when they died. It was a surreal experience. One that I, in retrospect, wish I had shared with my father and mother. But as my dad used to say, "Too soon we get old, too late we get smart." Looking back, I would have done things differently at the passing of my parents, but life just continues to be a learning experience.

Brenda and I have prepared for the future so that our children will not be burdened with expenses and planning after our eventual death. We will be cremated, and our remains will be placed in a niche of a mausoleum at Cedar Hill Cemetery in Hartford, Connecticut. We will be near the final resting place of Brenda's mother, father, and sister. We will be in good company with them and some of the most influential people in history who are buried there. God bless them all.

PARTING THOUGHTS

Once in a while, I come across an email that a friend has sent me and I love to share these with other friends. One such email that I received recently explores random thoughts that I think are both clever and funny. Following are some of those thoughts which I cannot take credit for along with others that I have come across in my lifetime. I hope you see the humor in what follows as much as I did.

So now cocaine is legal in Oregon, but straws aren't. That must be frustrating.

Still trying to wrap my head around the fact that 'Take Out' can mean food, dating, or murder!

Threw out my back sleeping and tweaked my neck sneezing, so I'm probably just one strong fart away from complete paralysis.

Dear paranoid people who check behind their shower curtains for murderers. If you do find one, what is your plan?

The older I get, the more I understand why roosters just scream to start their day.

Being popular on Facebook is like sitting at the 'cool table' in the cafeteria of a mental hospital.

I, too, was once a male trapped in a female body... but then my mother gave birth.

If only vegetables smelled as good as bacon.

When I lost the fingers on my right hand in a freak accident, I asked the doctor if I would still be able to write with it. He said, "Possibly, but I wouldn't count on it."

I woke up this morning determined to drink less, eat right, and exercise. But that was four hours ago when I was younger and full of hope.

Anyone who says their wedding was the best day of their life has never had two candy bars fall at once from a vending machine.

The biggest joke on mankind is that computers have begun asking humans to prove they aren't robots.

When a kid says, "Daddy, I want mommy," that's the kid's version of "I'd like to speak to your supervisor."

It's weird being the same age as old people.

Just once, I want a username and password prompt to respond CLOSE ENOUGH.

Last night the internet stopped working so I spent a few hours with my family. They seem like good people.

Weight loss goal: to be able to clip my toenails and breathe at the same time.

Now that COVID has everyone washing their hands correctly... next week... Turn Signals.

Someone said, "Nothing rhymes with orange." I said, "No, it doesn't."

The pessimist complains about the wind. The optimist expects it to change. The realist adjusts his sails.

An Aeronautical Engineer builds airplanes. A Civil Engineer builds targets.

There's a fine line between a numerator and a denominator. Only a fraction of people will find this funny.

I have many hidden talents. I just wish I could remember where I hid them.

Exercise helps you with decision-making. It's true. I went for a run this morning and decided I'm never going again.

The End

ABOUT THE AUTHOR

Richard (Dick) Stoebel was hit with the "writing bug" once again. Author of I'M ALMOST HISTORY and THE DEUCE COUPE THAT STOLE MY HEART, Dick reveals previously untold true stories that could only be written by someone who lived them. REAL SHORT STORIES is a vignette of events that spans from early childhood to retirement, and everywhere in between.

He grew up in a modest New England home, worked

during high school, married a beautiful woman, became an engineer working on jet engines, had two children, rebuilt old cars, and flew his own airplane.

His bucket list continues to check off items like flying a helicopter and doing aerobatics in a P51 Mustang. Future items include patenting an invention, cruising the Panama Canal, and living to see great grandchildren.

Now retired in Florida, Dick continues to enjoy the American dream. He hopes that you enjoy reading his book as much as he did writing it.

I'M ALMOST HISTORY

THE DEUCE COUPE THAT STOLE MY HEART